# At the
# CORE

# D. Allen

DN Publishing
–Since 2015–
DavidNethBooks.com

*At the Core*
Copyright © 2025 by D. Allen
Batavia, NY

www.DavidNethBooks.com



ISBN: 978-1-963602-38-8
First Edition

Subscribe to the author's newsletter for updates and exclusive content:
DavidNethBooks.com/Newsletter

Follow the author at:
www.facebook.com/DavidNethBooks
www.instagram.com/dnpublishing
www.patreon.com/dnpublishing

# Also by D. Allen

**Montana Beach**
Summer Stay

Summer Job

Summer Nights

**Small Town Christmas**
A Christmas Reunion

A Christmas Charade

A Christmas Spark

A Christmas Song

A Christmas Departure

A Christmas Wedding

A Christmas Escape

A Christmas Renovation

A Christmas Family

**Standalones**
Snow After Christmas

Thanksgiving Day Parade

At the Core

# Chapter One
## AUTUMN

I hauled the wooden apple crate out of the back of my truck and carried it down the slight slope on the sidewalk to the coffee shop. When nobody immediately came through the door, I propped the wooden box against my body using the brick wall of the shop for leverage and used my free hand to swing open the door. I stuck my foot out quickly to catch it so that I could step through once I got my hold back on the apple crate.

"Autumn, I could've helped you!" Hattie said once I stepped through the door. I squeezed around the glass display case that held the baked goods to hand her the crate on the other side.

When she took it from me, I felt immediate relief to have it off my hands. "It's okay. I managed." I tried not to show how out of breath I was. Maybe I needed to start running again? As if I had the time.

"This is heavy!" Hattie set it down on the floor and picked out what I had put inside back at the orchard. Three apple pies, a dozen apple cider donuts made fresh that morning, apple pie bars, and, of course, apples. Sometimes I was afraid that we had so many that we needed to give them away, but Grandma Wanda just found new ways to bake with them so we didn't have that problem.

"If you run out of this, I have plenty more back at the farm," I told her.

Hattie began to put them in the display case.

I leaned on the case as she worked, not wanting to rush her before I put in my coffee order. A lot of times, Hattie tried to give me the drink for free as a thank you for delivering the apples and the apple baked goods, but I always insisted on paying because I knew how businesses ran. You could only give out so many free things before you went bankrupt.

Once emptied, Hattie handed me back my crate, which I set on the floor beside me. "The usual?" she asked.

"Yes, please."

She moved right down the counter to start on my

drink. "How are things?"

The coffee shop was fairly quiet. It was a Monday afternoon at the end of summer, making it an off-peak time and season for them. Their busiest—pumpkin spice season—was just around the corner, and then I wouldn't have time to stop and visit. Truthfully, I didn't have time now, but I made the time for Hattie.

I sighed heavily. "Not great."

"Aw, things can't be that bad, can they?"

"Hattie, after I let you go I thought I would have some more cash flow month-to-month, but with the way that costs keep going up, I feel like I have *more* work to do and less money to make it work." I shook my head. "This is a lot harder than I thought."

Uncle Stan, Uncle Jim, and Dad were all left the farm by their father—my grandfather—who was the second-generation owner of Chapman Farms Family Orchards. For a while, the three of them ran it together. My parents ran the day-to-day operations of the orchard and everything on-site for customers while my Uncle Stan managed the cider portion of the business—both hard and sweet—while my Uncle Jim managed the wholesale part of the business—delivering to grocery stores and other third-party sellers, including being a major staple at farmer's markets across the region. After my parents passed away, I took on operations at the farm.

Hattie held the cup to the steamer and glanced over at me. "Being the boss is like that sometimes. Weren't you complaining that you wished you could make some of the decisions yourself?"

"Exactly! *Some* of the decisions. Not *all* of them!"

"You have your uncles and grandma to help make those decisions with you."

"Except for the fact that I'm driving the business into the ground, so they're probably not too happy with that," I said.

Hattie rolled her eyes as she wiped the stem of the steamer with a towel. "You're *not* running it into the ground!"

"Yes, I am," I insisted. "Big chunks of the business have been sold off and what's left of it might not be enough to sustain the business in today's world—maybe if we were operating in the 1800s again, but we're definitely *not* back then anymore."

Shortly after I took the place of my parents in the operation, Uncle Stan decided to close the cider portion of the business, citing difficulties keeping things in compliance with the health department. I knew what was really happening: it was costing too much and he wanted to sell it off while he still could.

Then, a few months ago my Uncle Jim decided to make a similar move and sell off the wholesale part of the business, which was a huge part of the overall business but one that took a toll on us logistically. Both sales ended up in a nice one-time payout for the business and for my uncles, but it also meant that they needed to find other full-time employment outside of the family business.

"And thank goodness for that," Hattie said. "Otherwise, there's no way that you, a woman, would be running the show." She handed me my drink.

I took it, feeling the liquid warm my fingers through the paper cup. "The truth is, if things don't turn up soon, I'm going to have to sell what's left of the business—or just close it altogether."

"No! You can't do that!"

The sale of the biggest parts of the business left me holding up the roof at Chapman Farms, trying to keep everything together while trying not to look at the writing on the wall. My uncles still each had one-third shares in what was left of the business, but they were mostly hands-off when it came to things outside of major business decisions.

In a sense, I was on my own.

I shrugged. "I don't really have a choice. It's not like I *want* to do that. It's my family's farm. It's where I grew up. It's where I still live. It's what's supported my family for generations and, thanks to me, that legacy is coming to an end. *My* legacy will be that I

am the reason a four-generation business closed its doors for good."

Hattie shook her head. "Don't put that on yourself. There are a lot more circumstances that go in to operating a business than just one person's business-savvy. There's the market, the economy, resources, community—so much!"

The bell above the door rang as another customer walked in. He stepped back and looked at the menu on the wall while we chatted.

"Well, I guess my pity party is over," I said. "I should let you get back to work. Thanks for listening—and let me know when you need me to bring more of those." I indicated the baked goods display case.

"I will! I'm sure they'll sell fast—they always do." Hattie smiled at me. "And good luck with everything. Let me know if there's anything I can do to help."

"Thanks. This apple season will certainly make or break me." With another wave, I stepped back out onto East Center Street and back to my truck.

# BRADEN

I carried my Starbucks coffee with me from my cubicle to the conference room, with my notepad and tablet tucked under my other arm.

"Hey, Clinton, did you do those stats for my monthly report?" Mr. Ramsey asked as he came out of his office. He always called me by my last name. I wasn't sure he even *knew* my first name.

"For July?" I asked.

"No, for January. Of course for July! What other month would I be talking about?"

I forced a laugh. Better to play the political game and be on the boss's good side. "Just finished going through them. I'll have them in your inbox by the end of the day."

Mr. Ramsey smacked me on the back and pulled me closer. I had to be careful not to spill my coffee all over him. "That's what I like to hear, sir! We need more people like you around here. Committed to their work."

*Devoted* to their work was more like it. I had been known to take work home and work on it until the late hours. Friday nights. Weekends. It didn't matter. I was like a Labrador retriever, desperate to please his master.

We stepped into the conference room and I was grateful to see that there were three other people there already. Not too many to make me feel like I was late, but not too early to force me to make any more small talk with my boss.

Ramsey nodded to the display screen mounted to the wall. "Pawlak, get this thing booted up for me." He handed off his laptop to our IT running man. As a recent graduate, Jon Pawlak was a young and energetic kid who always jumped at the chance to help someone.

That was probably why Mr. Ramsey liked him. I'd found that he liked to surround himself with Yes Men. I was very well aware that I was one of them as well.

Jon jumped up and began to get the technical equipment set up. I took a seat at the far end of the table, off to the side. Within line of sight of Mr. Ramsey as he talked at the head of the table, but not directly across from him. In the moment, it also helped me to blend in with the other early arrivals to the meeting.

While I waited, I logged on to my tablet and responded to a few work emails. I made sure to add a reminder to my task list to send Mr. Ramsey an email with the July numbers by the end of the day. Actually, I set the reminder for just after working

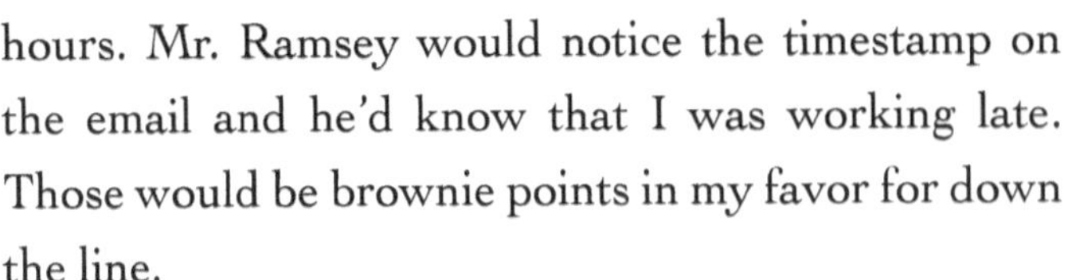



hours. Mr. Ramsey would notice the timestamp on the email and he'd know that I was working late. Those would be brownie points in my favor for down the line.

"All right, let's get started," Mr. Ramsey called.

I looked up from my tablet and saw that the table was crowded with people.

"I'm supposed to start off this meeting by reviewing our goals," he started. "But let me just tell you that we're kicking ass. Blossom Properties is growing *exponentially*. Our profits are through the roof as we expand into different markets."

By "expanding," he meant buying out properties that were in different markets and keeping their teams on as our employees so that the expertise would remain the same. It was a common business hack, although it didn't necessarily sit well with me considering that most of those entities that we bought up were small family businesses. Still, I was glad that I was on the winning side of that team.

"That's the good news," Mr. Ramsey continued. "The bad news is that we still haven't yet monopolized the apple market in Western New York, which makes any efforts to break into apple markets in other parts of the country difficult. And we should be able to! Easily!" His voice boomed throughout the room.

Love him or hate him, there was no denying that Mr. Ramsey could capture an audience. Granted, that was probably because he didn't ever let them speak, but still.

"I mean, take Chapman Farms up in Medina, for instance," he went on. "They've already sold off their cider business to us, which we've successfully relocated and repositioned to be a trending new hangout in Buffalo. It's doing well for us now that it's more centrally located."

His slick smile perfectly paired with the cold indifference of his words.

"And they just sold us their wholesale business, which we've picked up their operations and are working on incorporating into another avenue of our business." He paused and looked down at the table for dramatic effect. "Basically what I'm saying is that nobody can stop us. Blossom Properties is a force to be reckoned with in the food business." He held up a finger. "But there's still more to be done."

He turned to the screen that Jon Pawlak had loaded for him, indicating the graphs and charts that were displayed. "We counted that there are six other family-owned apple orchards in Western New York that are still operating on their own. My goal—no, *our* goal—is to bring them all under the Blossom Properties umbrella in the next two years. And that starts with Chapman Farms."

Mr. Ramsey snapped his fingers and pointed at me. "Clinton!"

I jumped, suddenly thrust in the spotlight of the room. "Ye-yes…sir."

*Sir*? Where the hell did that come from?

"You're going to start us on the path to greatness in Western New York. I want you to go to Chapman Farms and get them to sell the rest of the business to us. Pun fully intended here, but they should be low-hanging fruit. They're a dying business. I can't imagine it will take you very long to get them to sell. They're pretty desperate. Once we get them to sign, we'll be more intimidating to close in on some of those other family-owned orchards in the region."

I nodded dumbly, grasping around at my stuff to try to collect my things. Mr. Ramsey was a go-getter, so sometimes when he told us to do something, he meant for us to do it immediately. I didn't know if this was one of those times.

Mr. Ramsey waved me back in my seat. "I know you're eager, Clinton, but you can relax. Legal still needs to draft up the document you need to get them to sign before they throw even more paperwork at them to seal the deal."

I settled in my seat, relaxing at the prospect of not having to immediately come up with an answer for how to convince a long-standing family business to close.

"What's the matter, Clinton?" Mr. Ramsey asked, right in front of the whole room.

"Um…I'm just not sure…I don't—" A lack of confidence was the enemy in business, and that's exactly what I was showing.

"Pitch it as if you're doing them a favor," he said. "You're taking the burden of deciding off their hands. Highlight the payday for them. The get-rich quick scheme will secure the deal."

I nodded, still not sure that I would be able to do it. Sure, I had convinced other businesses to sell, but it was always cold and impersonal. And typically over the phone. Usually after a business had been handed down to multiple CEOs and the final one was just trying to staunch the financial bleeding and get out before an even bigger loss.

But a long-standing family-run business? That was different.

"Clinton," Mr. Ramsey called to me.

I looked up at him.

"If you pull this off, I'll have to start looking at a Director of Acquisitions position with your name all over it."

# AUTUMN

I ran a few more errands around town before heading back to the farm. On the rare days when I allowed myself to get away, I made the most of it and usually spent a good chunk of the day off the property. Most of my life nowadays revolved around the farm.

As I pulled back into the driveway, I saw a slick black sedan parked in our private driveway. Tinted windows. Waxed. Not a speck of dust or dirt on it.

The way the property was situated, we had a private driveway on one side of the house that was just for us, and there was a public parking lot on the other side of the house, which was pointed to the pole barn that had been put up in the last twenty years that was meant for the public. Additional fencing and greenery helped further define the boundary.

Still, sometimes people got confused.

I parked my truck in my usual spot and got out. I had a few bags of groceries in the back, but I left them where they were, opting instead to inspect the sedan.

The windows were nearly black, which didn't help alleviate my nerves at all. I considered finding a makeshift weapon, but figured I had enough space to

make an escape if there was someone nefarious inside. That was, if there even was *anyone* inside.

Turned out, there was.

The door opened and out stepped a man in a blue business suit and sunglasses. A curious thing, considering how tinted the windows in the car were.

"Hello." He removed his sunglasses and squinted against the late-summer sunlight.

I couldn't help but notice how out of place he looked, dressed the way he was. There was no way he could've been comfortable, considering how I was warm and I was in shorts made from cutoff jeans and a flannel with the sleeves rolled up.

Still, he did look sharp.

"I'm Braden Clinton. Are you the owner of Chapman Farms Family Orchards?" He offered his hand.

"I'm one of them." I shook his hand while eyeing him curiously. "I'm Autumn Chapman."

"Nice to meet you."

When my hand was freed, I crossed my arms. With the heat, it wasn't exactly comfortable, but it was more about conveying the symbol of hesitation than anything else.

"Can I help you with something?" I asked.

"Actually, there's something *I* can help *you* with." He offered a confident—cocky?—smile.

I raised my eyebrows.

"I'm the one who is going to save your family's business."

I shifted on my feet, becoming—if it was at all possible—even more skeptical. "Oh yeah? How exactly is that going to happen?"

"I'm going to buy your farm from you."

# Chapter Two
## AUTUMN

I looked this Braden What's-His-Name up and down as the hatred coursed through my veins. Who did this man think he was, coming to *my* property and telling me he was going to *help* me by taking my family's business off my hands? As if he was my knight in shining armor. As if I even needed that.

Truthfully, I *could* use help, but not by a total stranger. Braden Whatever-His-Name-Was.

Even though my blood was boiling, I kept my composure on the outside and held all my vicious words inside.

I met his eyes and simply said, "No, you're not." Then I turned and went back to my truck to retrieve my

grocery bags. By the time I turned around, he had followed me the short distance across the driveway.

His face showed genuine surprise.

I brushed past him and moved toward the house.

"Listen, I'm from Blossom Properties," he said, a little desperately now, "and I have an offer to purchase your business for a generous amount of money that would help save you from the financial strain you're under."

I stopped in my pursuit of the door and spun on my heels to face him. "The financial *strain* I'm under?"

Braden's confidence faltered further at my reaction.

"My *finances* are none of your business, stranger." I turned back around and fished in my pocket for my keys. I hoped I hadn't left them in the car. That would've been a walk of shame that I didn't need. Not in this moment.

"You don't even want to look at the offer?" he asked.

I looked up at him again. "Okay. Let me say this *again*, because either I'm being unclear or you're just stupid—" So much for keeping my composure. "— but listen to the words that are coming out of my mouth." I pointed to my lips for further effect. "I. Am. Not. Selling."

I finally found my keys and tried to balance my shopping bags on my arm while I located the right key.

"Miss Chapman—Autumn, if I may—with all due respect, our company has presented this offer to you because we love the business that you've created and we want to help it excel at the next level."

I spun around again. "See, what you don't seem to be getting is that you don't see anything wrong with just showing up at my *home* unannounced to *tell* me that I'm supposedly going to do something that I don't even *want* to do, without even giving me any valid reasons as to why your company could do any better at running my family's business than me. I mean, who does that?"

He opened his mouth to respond, but I cut him off.

"I'll tell you who. Only someone who is so far removed from reality that they can't see how *rude* that is." I shook my head. "Even if I was considering selling the business, I certainly wouldn't sell it to someone like *you*."

"Okay, okay." He held his hands out, trying to calm me down. It only made me angrier that he was, yet again, trying to control me. Who did this guy think he was? And where the hell did he come from?

"I understand that this is an emotional decision

and you need time to sit with it for a minute before you—"

"You're not hearing me!" I shouted, despite myself. "I'm not selling. So now you are left with two options: you can get the hell off my property, or I'll give you a reason to get off my property."

I unlocked the door, stepped inside to the sound of Grandma Wanda's dog, Maggie, barking in the next room, and set the bags down on a chair beside the door.

Braden persisted on the other side of the screen door. "I see that you're busy. Is there a better time that I can come back for us to discuss this further?"

I looked at him through the screen. "How's this? I'll give you two minutes until I see your car heading back to the road. If not, then I'll come back out with my grandfather's gun."

His BB gun, but a gun nonetheless.

"Got it?" I pressed.

The sense of fear that I was shooting for never really reached Braden's eyes, but my threat had the effect that I wanted. He backed away with his arms up in surrender.

Seeing his retreat, I slammed the front door shut and went back into the house. With any luck, I'd never see that man again in my life.

# Chapter Three

## BRADEN

I wasn't sure I was going to be able to return to work. But, like any other professional, I sucked it up and faced the music. If Mr. Ramsey asked—*when* Mr. Ramsey asked—to see the contract that I was supposed to so easily get a signature on, I would be honest with him and tell him that things hadn't gone according to plan. And if anyone else gave me a hard time about it, I would ignore them. The only opinion that mattered to me was my boss's.

I just wished I believed half the crap I told myself.

My *real* strategy was to arrive early, before anyone else, so I could avoid the scrutiny of everyone else asking if I had been able to deliver on the boss's special task.

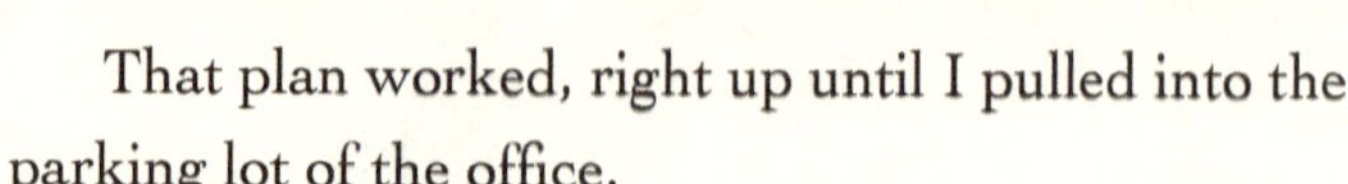

That plan worked, right up until I pulled into the parking lot of the office.

"Clinton!" Ivan Montgomery cheered when he saw me. "Look at you coming in early!" He had his messenger bag slung over his shoulder and he carried his coffee with one hand while he fumbled with his keys in the other.

I offered a polite smile, searching my brain for any excuse to slow my progress into the building so I didn't have to walk in with him. Since I had already left my car when he called my name and there were no other distractions between my car and the door, I came up empty.

"Yeah, I thought I might get a jumpstart on some stuff," I offered.

We walked up the tiny sidewalk path to the unassuming side door of the office building. It was a one-story building surrounded by a sea of asphalt, neighboring four other buildings that looked otherwise exactly the same. If it wasn't for the address and company logo printed on to the glass on the main door, nobody would ever be able to distinguish each building apart.

Efficiency at its finest.

"How'd you make out at Chapman Farms yesterday?" He held the door open for me and I stepped through.

I cleared my throat. "Well…there's been a development with that, so I'm going to need to talk to Mr. Ramsey about it today."

Montgomery wasn't buying it. "You weren't able to get them to sign."

"It's a long-standing family business and—"

"And we buy up businesses and properties like that all the time." We stopped at an intersection of cubicle pathways, where we needed to part ways. He adjusted the strap on his shoulder. "Look, all I'm saying is that if you want that position that Ramsey promised you yesterday, you can't make this personal. It's just business. So go out there and get the account!"

I nodded. "You're right. I will."

We parted and I gratefully went to my desk, away from any other criticism. Montgomery's pep talk was nice. He had a point. I couldn't be a sucker for sob stories. Not if I was going to make it in business.

But I couldn't help but remember the flowers outside the Chapman house. It was homey. And relaxing. And *comfortable*. Not anything like the stark, fluorescent-light-filled blandness that was my office building. Of course, why would we *need* anything other than a building with the essential utilities to get work done?

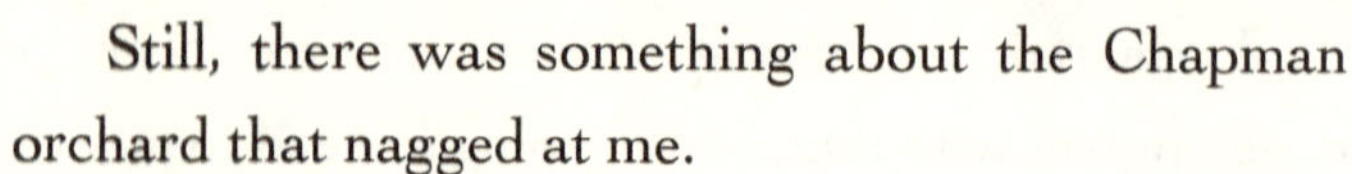



Still, there was something about the Chapman orchard that nagged at me.

Mr. Ramsey showed up about a half an hour after I arrived at the office. He was one that always made his presence known with how loud his voice was. Even when he wasn't necessarily yelling, his raspy voice carried across all the cubicles in the office.

"Marge! You look nice today, honey!"

"Tony! How are the kids doing? Those little rugrats eating you out of house and home yet?"

"How about them Bills?"

Things of that nature could be heard from him whenever he arrived at the office.

Today was no different.

"Clinton! You're here early."

I looked up and saw him at the edge of the cubicle area.

He nodded toward his space. "My office."

My nerves began to mount as I rose and followed him into his office. I could almost feel all the eyes on me coming from the cubicles as I passed by.

The bookshelves behind Mr. Ramsey's desk were filled with everything but books. Pictures of his kids. Diplomas. Certificates of completion. Succulents. Bills memorabilia. All of it added up to a mixture of all the parts of Mr. Ramsey's very loud personality.

"Take a seat, Clinton." He motioned to the two

chairs in front of his desk and powered up his computer. He reached for his coffee and sat back in his chair. "Do you have the contract?"

"Uh…well…not exactly." My throat was suddenly very dry. "Autumn Chapman, the owner, she, uh—"

"Did she give you a hard time?" Mr. Ramsey smirked.

I sighed, relieved that he didn't make me say it. "Yeah. She was very opposed to the idea of selling and was very turned off to the fact that I showed up to her house to make the offer."

He waved off the idea and turned back to his computer to log in. "That's just her pride talking. You stay on her—don't let her win. Sooner or later, you'll wear her down." He turned his attention fully to his computer, signifying that the conversation was over.

"So…how long should I keep trying before I give up?"

That got his attention. He turned and pointed a finger at me. "Don't ever give up. If you learn nothing else from me, that's what I want you to understand. The defining factor that any successful businessman has is persistence. The longer you stay on something, sooner or later, you're going to see some wins. As for this case…" He rocked his head back and forth. "It is probably a good idea to put a deadline on the deal to convince her to sell. Can't let her think that this option is always open." He rubbed his chin and looked up toward the ceiling.

I sat there, debating when would be a good expiration date for the offer. However, I was also trying to determine if this was a two-person conversation or if Mr. Ramsey just wanted to think out loud.

"She's going to be pretty upset by her profits now that the other parts of the business are gone," he ruminated. "And the business is going to be in flux, as far as finances, while they try to downgrade while keeping up their status with their customer base. This year is really going to be the deciding factor so…" He snapped his fingers and pointed at me again. "You stay on her until the end of the apple season. If she doesn't sell before then, there's no doubt that she will after their largest money-making season is over and they don't have enough to cover their costs. They'll be *begging* us for a buyout!" He smiled, amused by that idea.

I nodded. "So the beginning of November?"

Mr. Ramsey gave a curt nod, any humor on his face suddenly gone. "November first, not a day later. If she turns out to be that stubborn and still hasn't sold by then, we can pick up the farm and its assets at auction when they inevitably go out of business.

We'll get them one way or another. Don't you worry about that."

Not sure what else to say, I nodded and stood. "Okay. I'll do that. Thank you, sir."

"No problem, Clinton. You'll get that account." He said it with such assurance. "Show those country bumpkins why we're the sharks in this business. And remember, Director of Acquisitions sounds pretty good, doesn't it?"

"I'll do what I can," I told him.

I left his office feeling mixed emotions. Chapman Farms was a family business, as in a *family* still lived on the property and ran it. And Blossom Properties, the soulless entity that pretended to have character, was going to buy it out and take away yet another nostalgic icon in our area. Personally, I hated that.

But I couldn't think about that. Ivan was right. I couldn't make this personal. It was business. I had a job to do, and if I was successful, I was going to be paid handsomely for it.

# Chapter Four
## AUTUMN

Sunday family dinners have always been my favorite. Back when I was growing up, they used to happen every week. My parents and I lived in the large family home with Grandma Wanda and Grandpa Frank, while my Uncle Stan and Aunt Jeanine lived in the farmhouse of a neighboring farm we had bought when the orchard needed to expand and Uncle Jim lived in a small cottage deeper in the field. That was before he married Aunt Cheryl. My dad used to joke that he wouldn't ever meet anyone living deep in the orchard property by himself. It still makes me smile to remember the look on my dad's and Uncle Stan's faces when Uncle Jim first brought Aunt Cheryl around.

They were so surprised!

Of course, after the car accident that took my parents, and now that both of my uncles were married with young families, Sunday family dinners happened less and less often. Which made each one even more special.

Grandma Wanda still insisted on making dinner for everyone tonight—a big bowl of pasta that could easily go around to all eleven of us—all five of my cousins, me, both my uncles, both my aunts, and my grandma.

With that many people seated around the dinner table, it was really no surprise that the volume of the house increased tenfold. So when dinner was over and both Aunt Jeanine and Aunt Cheryl began to clean up the dishes, they sent my younger cousins outside to play, which was when I got the first inclination that tonight's Sunday dinner was an elaborate hoax meant to disguise an intervention.

Uncle Jim moved from the head of the table to sit beside Uncle Stan. Grandma Wanda stayed where she was at the other end of the table. Even though I couldn't see it, I knew that her dog Maggie was curled up at her feet.

Nobody talked at first, bringing the joyful nature of the family dinner down to a much more somber one.

"Autumn," Uncle Stan started. "We wanted to talk

to you about the farm's finances."

My heart began to race, but I kept a casual stance, slouched in my seat. Was it obvious that my whole body had gone rigid?

"We think it's time that you got serious about this," Uncle Jim said.

"About the farm's finances?" I asked. "I'm very serious about it. I know where things stand." In fact, I often lost sleep over the direction the farm was heading in under my guidance.

"Knowing where things stand and knowing how to operate a business are two different things," Uncle Stan said gently. His voice was usually very deep and booming—he used to scare me when I was little when he would raise his voice even a little bit. At the moment, I knew he was holding back. Treating me with kid gloves.

I shrugged. "Do you want me to consult with a professional or something? Or are you guys going to be more active in the business? I mean, what exactly is this?"

"Someone from Blossom Properties has reached out to each of us about selling our shares of the business," Uncle Jim explained.

I had a newfound hatred for Braden What's-His-Name. How dare he go to my uncles and try to pester them to sell!

Then again, the way I had acted when he came to the house replayed in my mind. It wasn't my finest hour. In fact, I didn't recognize the person that I was then. I was in a very defensive mode, with my family's livelihood and homestead being threatened, and Braden was the easiest outlet.

Of course, the fact that he went behind my back to my uncles showed that not only was he *trying* to take our business from us, he was intent on succeeding in it.

"And…we're considering the offer," Uncle Jim continued.

My body lurched forward and I grabbed the table with both hands. "You can't!"

Maggie began barking at my outburst.

"Hush, honey," Grandma Wanda murmured to her dog under the table.

"Autumn, how can we not?" Uncle Stan asked. "It's not our first choice, no, but we have to be realistic here. The family has changed, the business has changed, the *market* has changed, and so has the economy. The fact of the matter is, our farm is failing. And if we don't sell now, there might not be another buyout offer again, and all of us might never financially recover from it."

I shook my head, firmly digging my heels into the proverbial ground. "No. No, we can't sell! This is—" I stopped and adjusted my position mid-argument. It helped that Maggie came over and hopped into my lap. "—*your* grandfather built this business when he first came to this country. Selling it would be like spitting on his grave."

"Autumn, you know that's not what we're trying to do." Uncle Stan's scary voice was coming out, but my frustration—my *desperation*—was in full control now.

"This is the house you grew up in—it's the house *I* get up in. The only place I've ever lived! I used to be the water runner when you were out working in the orchard, running up and down the rows of trees to get you guys water in the middle of summer. You both used to drive the trucks with Dad to deliver apples all over the area. We used to do family bonfires outside in the fall. This place has history—*our* history. We can't just sell it off for the highest dollar."

Both of my uncles were quiet, but I could see Uncle Jim softening.

"This property is owned free and clear, which has been a huge help for us financially," he said.

Uncle Stan, however, was having none of that. He shook his head. "No. No! We can't keep making decisions based on sentiment and nostalgia. That's how we got where we are to begin with. Something needs to change."

Maggie let out a warning bark, which I appreciated.

Uncle Stan was by no means the decider in the family, but he did have a tendency of using his big voice and status as the oldest brother—now that Dad was gone—to assert his opinions as facts. But there was a trump card that hadn't been played yet.

"Grandma! You can't let them force me to sell!" I hated the emotion that made its way to my voice, but I was desperate. Even Maggie was restless in my lap. She kept spinning in circles, unable to lay down until the tension dissipated.

Both Uncle Stan and Uncle Jim fell quiet as they waited for their mother's response.

Grandma Wanda didn't make an effort to speak at first. Her face remained neutral, impossible to tell what she was thinking.

"I've lived on this farm for more than sixty years," she finally said. "I've seen how hard our family has worked to make this land—*our* land—provide for us. And it has. Listen, I've been through it all, from when your daddy—" She leaned over to me. "—your granddaddy—was just a worker on his father's farm to running it himself, and eventually passing it on to you kids. Now, I won't sit here and pretend that I'm glad that Paul's not with us anymore, but I will say that I'm very happy that a *fourth* generation of Chapmans are now in charge of this estate."

"That's nice, Ma, but that's not going to pay the bills," Uncle Stan countered, but Grandma Wanda put up her finger to his face.

"Don't interrupt me. I'm getting there." She waited for complete silence, save for my aunts' chitchat in the kitchen, before continuing. "Now, I don't want to see this farm go anymore than Autumn does—and I know you boys don't want that, either! And I can see where the two of you are coming from, but you have to give Autumn a chance. She just took it over last year, just before apple season, so last year's profits weren't what we'd hoped they'd be. And then with selling off another major part of the business, our farm is changing and not everything has settled yet to make a sound decision on whether it has the capacity to stay open or not."

There was hope. I could feel it. It wasn't a silver bullet by any means, but it was something.

"I'm trying," I offered. "I really am."

Uncle Jim nodded. "I know that, sweetheart. I know."

"Now, I'm willing to help out in any way that I can," Grandma Wanda offered. "But I know that these types of offers are not going to be around forever. Like I said, as much as I don't want to sell, I

think it's best that we set a deadline to determine whether that's our next logical step. One that gives Autumn a fair chance to put us in a place that will carry us for generations to come."

A tall order that I wasn't sure I could even deliver on, but it was the chance that I had been fighting for.

Uncle Stan sighed heavily, clearly not happy with the decision. Still, he relented. "Okay. We'll give you until the end of this apple season to turn things around. Come winter, if we're not turning enough of a profit to stay open, then we'll have no choice but to go to Blossom Properties and sell the farm."

# Chapter Five
## BRADEN

At first, driving into Medina from the south was like every other Western New York town. The large corporate commercial businesses bombarded drivers, demanding their attention with drive-thrus, signs, and other pleas for sales. Dunkin' Donuts, Walgreens, a forgotten motel, and a large gas station sat on the busy corner just before entering the village — and that wasn't to forget the large car dealership.

But very quickly, the village turned pretty quintessential with beautiful large street trees, well-maintained sidewalks, and perfectly preserved houses that, I was sure, had sat at their locations for years. Sure, there were the cracks and flaws here and there, but that

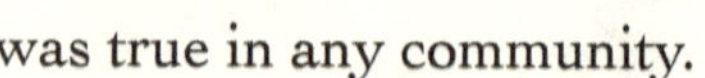



was true in any community.

Those were all details I hadn't noticed the first time I had driven through Medina. I had been on a mission before for a quick sale. Now, I was geared up for a marathon of persistence.

As I came up to the downtown area, it was as if the town was straight out of a postcard. Beautiful old brick buildings lined the street, with angled parking, bountiful flowers, and—what was most surprising— people actually walking up and down the sidewalk at all the different specialty shops. The baker, the bookstore, the florist, the coffee shop, the candy store. All of it together created the cute little town that seemed as if it was straight out of a Hallmark movie.

Sara always liked Hallmark movies.

I turned down West Center Street, which had even more storefronts. I pulled into a parking lot beside the small farmer's market office, and across the street from a retro 1950s diner.

Did this town ever relent on the cuteness?

I reached in the backseat for my bag, but stopped when my phone rang.

Lenny.

He was my brother-in-law, or rather my *former* brother-in-law now that Sara was gone. Since it had been just Lenny and Sara growing up, he and I had

grown close over the duration of my time with Sara. Even with her gone, we still checked in on one another.

"Hey, Lenny," I said into the phone.

"Brady! How are things?"

*Brady.* I hadn't been called that since high school. But, old habits died hard with old friends.

"They're okay," I replied. "How are the kids?" Lenny had two kids with his wife, Bernice. A boy and a girl, just like him and Sara. Funny how ironic fate was.

"They're good. Bernie is counting down the days until school starts again."

I scrunched my brow, trying to think of the calendar. It was the end of August, which meant that the school year would be starting soon. It hadn't been on my radar. September didn't mean much when you didn't have kids.

"That's gotta be coming soon." I didn't know what else to say to that.

"Tuesday."

"Oh wow," I said. "Really soon, then. So she only has a few more days with them.

"Yeah, they go back the day after Labor Day," Lenny said. "Speaking of, do you have any plans for this weekend?"

I eyed up the brick building I was parked next to.

Online it claimed that there was a small hotel in it, but it didn't look like any hotel I'd ever stayed at. Sure, there was a national chain on the edge of town that I could've chosen, but I thought a locally owned one right in town would help me get a better feel for the town. Maybe pick up on the public perception of Chapman Farms to give me better insight into my persuasion techniques.

In my silence, Lenny filled the void in conversation. "We're just having one last cookout before the kids go back to school and we start getting into the weekly grind. Nothing big. Just my parents and some of the neighbors. Maybe a total of, like, fifteen people, including me, Bernie, and the kids."

I shifted in my seat, feeling a mix of emotions. On the one hand, I didn't want to disappoint Lenny and Bernie. They had been very supportive of me after I lost Sara, and still continued to consider me part of the family. But on the other hand, pretending to still be a part of that family when I very clearly *wasn't* was not a comfortable experience for me. Every moment I was with them, I would be thinking about Sara and everything she was missing out on. I would be thinking about how unfair it was that I got to see Lenny's kids grow up and not Sara, who loved them as if they were her own. Our own.

"I don't know, Len," I started.

"Well, the invitation still stands, as always," he said, giving me an out. "We'd love to see you. The kids have been asking about you."

I doubted that was true. At five and three years old, Henry and Eva were naturally self-involved and only thought of others when it directly impacted them.

"It's just that we haven't seen you all summer, and this is the perfect noncommittal weekend everyone seems to have," Lenny went on. "Even if you just drop in for an hour, that'd be fine."

"I'll let you know." I was fully intending to "forget" to text him. "I'm actually working on securing a really big account right now and the owner is being kind of stubborn about it so I was planning on spending this weekend putting pressure on her."

"Over a holiday weekend?"

"Well, it's a farm, so that doesn't really matter to them."

"True. What account is it?"

"Chapman Farms Family Orchards. They're up in Medina, which is actually where I am now."

"Never heard of them," Lenny said. "But then, why would I?"

"They used to make hard cider, but we bought that part of their business out already. I'm trying to secure the rest of the farm, but the owner's being a real bitch. You actually had some of their cider the last time we had dinner." I tried to remember when exactly that was—last spring, maybe?

"Oh, right. Well, hey, even if you can't make it out this weekend, consider stopping out for Henry's birthday party in a couple weeks."

"Wow," I said. "Hard to believe he's going to be six already." It was an attempt to divert the conversation away from his invitation. "I remember when he was first born. Hell, I remember when you and Bernie were just getting married and there *weren't* any kids yet."

"I know. It goes quick," he said. "So, can we count on you?"

"I'll have to check my calendar." When it came to the kids, I almost always caved.

"Great! I'll text you the details. You should also consider spending the holidays with us."

"The holidays? Lenny, it's not even September."

"September is in just a few short days—"

"Technically, these are some of the *longest* days of the year," I cut in, trying to add some levity to our conversation. I valued Lenny's friendship, but seeing him brought back memories I wasn't ready to unpack yet.

"And they're getting shorter," Lenny said. "Either

way, whether it's Thanksgiving or Christmas or both, we'd like to have you join us. I think the plan is just to have my parents and you. You can invite your folks, too, if you want. Just let Bernie know who is coming so she can plan the food."

I nodded, trying to figure out a polite way to get him off the phone before I had to turn down anymore invitations.

"Yeah, I'll let you know," I said quickly. "Look, I want to get checked into this hotel so I can make sure I have a room. I'll talk to you later."

"Text me about this weekend," Lenny said. "Like I said, even if it's just for an hour, we'd love to see you. And don't forget to check about Henry's birthday."

"Will do. See you, Len. Tell Bernie and the kids I said hi."

With him off the phone, I felt a sinking dread in the pit of my stomach. How much longer would I be able to turn down his invitations before he stopped asking me altogether? And how would I explain my reservations about seeing Sara's family to little Henry?

To distract my mind, I grabbed my bag and got out of my car. I walked up to the sidewalk and looked at the signs above the doors until I saw the one for the small boutique hotel. I walked up, hearing the ring of the antique bell above the door.

Seriously, did this town ever skimp on the charm?

The lobby of the hotel was more of a foyer entryway to several other businesses. To the left looked like it led to a storage room of sorts—maybe a brewery?—and to the right led to a restaurant and bar. A large set of stairs took up most of the lobby space, while the desk for the hotel was shoved to the back on the left.

A man a few years older than me popped his head out of a doorway a few feet behind the small hotel desk. "Hi there. Can I help direct you?"

"Well, that depends," I said. "Can you help me book a room for the hotel?"

His eyes seemed to light up a little. "Oh, yes! Do you need any special accommodations?" He stepped up to a laptop and began plugging in his login information.

I set my bag on the floor by my feet. "I saw online that you have some suites available. Could I snag one of those? It doesn't need to be large or anything. Maybe a studio. It's just me."

The man nodded. "Certainly." He extended his hand. "I'm Micah. Micah Thomas. I'm the manager of the hotel."

"Braden," I offered.

He looked down at his computer. "We have a studio suite available."

"That works."

"How long will you be staying?"

"Do you offer extended stays?"

"Sure we do. We offer by the week, or by the month, depending on your plans."

"Can I do one month?" I had decided on the way up to Medina that I'd better have a place to stay in case Autumn Chapman gave me a hard time. Or, if worse came to worst, and I failed at convincing her to sell. I could extend my stay longer if I needed.

"Certainly," Micah said. He gave me the price, which clearly reflected the long stay, but was also cheaper than I had thought it would be.

I swiped my credit card, grabbed a receipt for the tax write-off, then followed Micah up the creaky stairs to the third floor, where he led me to a room at the end of the short landing.

The room was small—clearly built at a time before modern building codes—but it had a lot of charm. The wood floors creaked even worse up here. There was a small wall of cabinetry that made up the kitchenette to the right, with a small round dining table next to it, beside a window. To the left was a queen-sized bed tucked in a little nook between the brick exterior wall and some built-in closet cabinets.

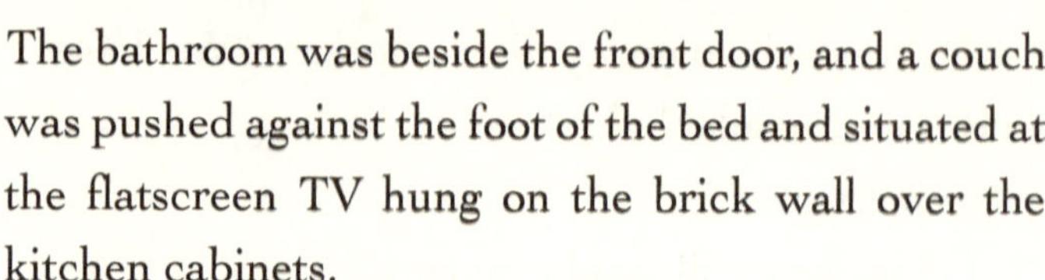



The bathroom was beside the front door, and a couch was pushed against the foot of the bed and situated at the flatscreen TV hung on the brick wall over the kitchen cabinets.

The best feature of all, though, were the extra-tall windows that let in a lot of natural light and looked out at the village below.

"Is this to your liking?" Micah asked.

"This will do just fine, thank you," I said.

"If you need anything, you can find me or someone else down at the front desk. If nobody's there, there's an emergency number on the sheet over on the kitchen counter."

He pointed and I looked over to see a laminated paper on the marble counter.

"Got it. Thank you."

Micah left and I walked up to the windows to take in the view. I was filled with that melancholy feeling again. It was beautiful, but I was ashamed of the reason I was there—to destroy a portion of this small town charm.

What made me even sadder, though, was the thought of how much Sara would've loved this place if she were still alive.

# Chapter Six
## BRADEN

Labor Day weekend was a boon for Chapman Farms because when I pulled up, there were several other cars in the parking lot. Whole families were lining up to buy bags to go apple picking. Twenty-something girls were huddling together in front of apple trees to take pictures in their flannels, as if it hadn't just been eighty degrees a week ago. The roar of a tractor sounded in the distance as it moved a large wooden crate of apples from within the orchard.

I got out of the car—this time, more casually dressed, albeit I was still in a dress shirt and black slacks. I needed to convey some level of authority. At the very least, I had rolled up my sleeves. That was casual, right?

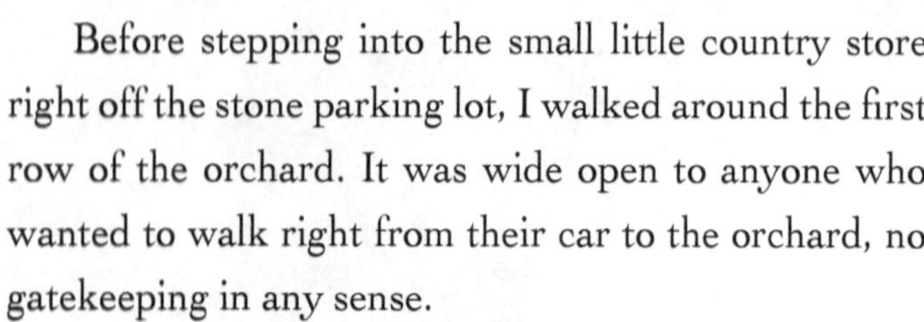



Before stepping into the small little country store right off the stone parking lot, I walked around the first row of the orchard. It was wide open to anyone who wanted to walk right from their car to the orchard, no gatekeeping in any sense.

As I wandered, I examined a few apples and tried to eavesdrop on some of the conversations of the customers. I was hoping to get a feel for the public perception of the business, to further give me insight into how I could approach the sales pitch.

"I *love* it here!" one girl exclaimed. She was in a red plaid flannel, jeans, boots, and an obnoxiously wide-brimmed hat.

"I know, but there are a lot of rows that aren't ready yet," her friend said, who sported an aptly named "shacket" that had already been tied around her waist in the heat.

Together, the two of them walked down the row of trees carrying a tiny plastic bag that was only half-filled with apples.

"It's still early," Flannel Girl said.

"Yeah, I just wish they had more."

"It's apple picking, what else do you need?"

"Ugh, I don't even know. I just…I mean, we're going to be here for, what, like thirty minutes tops? And then it's over. I don't know. I just thought we could make a day of it, but there's not really anything here."

I looked around. Shacket Girl was right. Sure, the orchard had the cutesy country store, but otherwise they didn't have anything else. No stacks of hay bales for ambiance, no mums, no pumpkins — nothing to fully satisfy the "fall vibe" dreams of customers.

Looked like Mr. Ramsey was right. Chapman Farms was a ship sinking fast.

I ventured back over to the parking lot, where I noticed that my brown leather shoes were wet with dew from the grass. I hadn't thought about that. I knelt down and tried to wipe away the dampness with my hand as best as I could.

"You're in the country now, city boy," a familiar voice said from behind me.

I straightened and saw Autumn walking along the row of trees with a wooden sign tucked under her arm and a hammer in the other hand.

"Admit it, though. You missed me." I offered her a teasing smile. If I came on as strong and confident as I had the last time I was here, she'd go into defensive mode and wouldn't listen to anything, even reason. My new plan: get her to like me. And be persistent.

Autumn rolled her eyes and kept walking. "I thought I told you to get out of here?" She stepped to the side of the country store building and lined up the

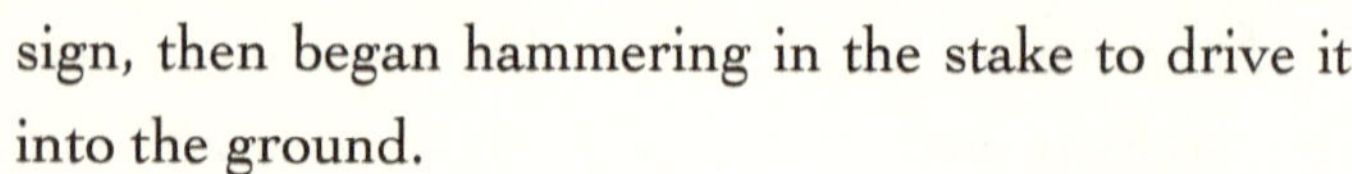



sign, then began hammering in the stake to drive it into the ground.

I walked up and read the sign aloud. "Please purchase bags first." I looked up at her with raised eyebrows. "Having trouble with thefts?"

"More like loiterers," she said. "People come for the pictures, then leave. This isn't a pretty backdrop, this is a business."

"You ever think the problem is that the row of apple trees butts right up against the parking lot?"

She nodded. "Oh! You're right, I'll get started on moving that row of apple trees this afternoon." She rolled her eyes again and then spun around to enter the store.

"I mean it." I followed her in. "Consider putting in a fence or something to help direct people into the store. It'll work better than the sign."

The store had that sweet apple smell to it that brought back a rush of nostalgia for me. At least Chapman Farms had that going for it. There was a long checkout counter along one wall, with a door behind the counter that led into an adjacent building. The store wasn't huge, but it was well-stocked with jams, jellies, bins of apples, and other country store offerings. Cute knickknack signs filled one wall, while a large bakery display cut into the long checkout counter. Another door toward the back of the store led out to the orchard, but it was blocked by baskets containing baking mixes.

Despite all of its offerings, though, the store was empty.

"Oh wow," I said without even realizing it. "This is...*nice*!"

Autumn walked behind the counter. "You sound surprised."

I shrugged. "I guess I shouldn't be, but I wasn't expecting to see such a well-stocked store."

"We respond to our customers' interests," she said.

"And yet you haven't picked up on the fact that you might not want to block that door that leads out to the orchard? That way people could go right outside after they buy their bags." Why did I keep offering her advice? I was supposed to be buying her business from her, not helping her improve it.

Autumn crossed her arms. "Well, while listening to your criticisms has been *fun*, I have work to do, so if you'll excuse me I have *actual* customers to take care of."

I resisted the urge to point out the empty store. Instead, I glanced over at the baked goods display. "Those cinnamon apple muffins look good. I'll take one of those."

She raised her eyebrows. "I don't need your pity."

I put up my hands in surrender. "What pity?"

"If you're just buying a three dollar muffin from me to make it look like you're being supportive and disarming, then you can take those three singles and shove them—"

"Hey, I just haven't had any breakfast yet this morning."

She looked down at my trim waist, then back up at me. "And you're telling me you usually get your breakfast at the bakery? You look like someone who chugs a protein shake on his way into work straight from the gym, then picks up a coffee at some chain place so that you can blend in with all the other basic suits you work with."

I forced myself to remain expressionless as she hurled insults at me. Completely accurate assumptions, but insults nonetheless. When she was done, I pointed to the display and asked, "So…that muffin?"

Her voice contorted in rage as she poised to throw even more vitriol my way. "You—"

The door opened and a young family walked in, with two kids running in excitedly.

"I'll be out your way in just a minute," I told them. "I'm just getting a muffin."

Autumn glared at me, but she retrieved a muffin for me and tossed it into a bag. She punched the keys

in the cash register—which was probably new in 1988—and said, "That'll be six-fifty."

"I thought you said…" I shook my head. "Never mind. Do you take card or cash?"

"I'd prefer cash."

Of course she would. No credit card fee then. I pulled my wallet out of my pocket and handed her a ten. "Keep the change."

"No thanks." She quickly tried to make my change, but I was already walking away.

"I can't wait to have this." I held up the bag as I backed up toward the door. "I'm sure it's delicious."

"Wait! I have your change!" She held it up, but the coins slipped out of her hand and bounced off the counter. When it rolled on the floor, one of the kids chased after it.

"Good luck with business today." I gave her a friendly wave and a smile and quickly left before we fell into another argument.

I still didn't have a signed contract, but I felt good about my stop in. Director of Acquisitions, I was on my way! Like Mr. Ramsey said, I would wear her down with my charm. And, it seemed, I was going to have a little fun doing it too.

# Chapter Seven
## AUTUMN

It was evening and we had officially closed for the day, which meant I could actually get to work on sprucing up the farm for the—hopefully—really big crowd that would come later in the fall. It was still early September and the heat hadn't yet relented. I knew from years of experience that once we got one chilly weekend that dipped into the sixties or even the fifties, we'd have crowds coming in waves to get their apples and other apple products.

At least, that's what I hoped would happen.

With all the cars cleared, I stood in the parking lot while the dump truck backed up and deposited the stone into some of the larger holes that had been worn away

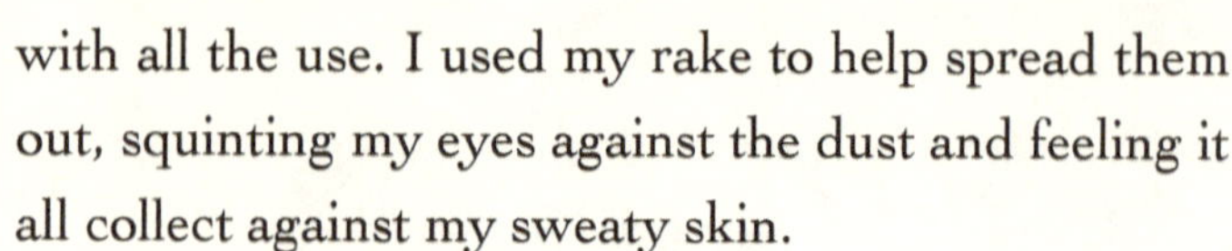



with all the use. I used my rake to help spread them out, squinting my eyes against the dust and feeling it all collect against my sweaty skin.

After turning off the truck, Tom Saunders came over to help spread out the load, but I waved him off. "I've got it. You can run home to your wife. I know you made a special delivery for me with this, and I appreciate it."

"Are you sure?"

I nodded again, continuing my work at spreading out the stone. "I mean it, Tom. Get out of here. I appreciate it. Send me a bill in the mail and I'll write you a check."

"Look, Autumn…consider this one on me."

I stopped what I was doing and leaned on my rake. "Are you trying to give me charity?"

Tom stammered. "No. It's just that…I know how things can be. I know you're in a tough situation right now."

He was an old family friend who lived around the corner. He had been supplying landscaping supplies to the farm for years. Back in the day, it was a partnership between two family businesses. Years ago, though, Tom's father sold the business. The family was retained as employees, but the base of the operations moved out toward Buffalo more—along with the decision-making, which included whether to give a family friend a donation.

"And where did you hear that from?" I demanded.

"Look, Autumn, I'm not trying to offend you. I just thought..."

"Thanks for delivering the stone, Tom." I went back to my work. "I'll be waiting for your invoice. If I don't get one, I'll send you a check based on last year's invoice."

I tried not to show how annoyed I was, even though I knew it was probably obvious. Had my uncles been talking about me? I knew they were buddies with Tom, being around the same age and all. I only hoped word hadn't spread to the rest of Medina. I didn't need charity customers, and I didn't need word to spread that I wasn't doing well as a boss. That would ruin the reputation of Chapman Farms and, as it was, that reputation was exactly what I was relying on to get through this apple season—and probably the next. If there would even be a next one.

Tom nodded, conceding. "You have a good day, then."

As Tom's dump truck pulled out of the parking lot, I raced against the dwindling daylight to get the work done. Sure, I could've put on the floodlights outside the house, but that would've left shadows on the ground from the trees and it wouldn't have been ideal working conditions.

It wasn't long before I noticed the headlights coming up the driveway. That damn black car.

Braden Clinton.

I stood with my rake propped against the ground and glared at his tinted windshield, knowing full-well who was behind it.

Sure enough, he climbed out of the car, dressed in shiny brown penny loafers, black pants, and a crisp powder-blue dress shirt. The sleeves were rolled up to convey a level of casualness, but the way they were so precisely rolled told me that he had inspected himself in the mirror before going out in public.

"Well, aren't you just a ray of sunshine!" he said once he was out of the car.

"We're closed."

"Not for good, I hope," he said. "Not if I can help it."

"What do you want?" I turned back to continue working, trying to show him how uninterested I was in him.

"I was hoping to get some of that apple butter I saw in the store the other day, but if it's past closing time I suppose I can come back tomorrow."

I sighed heavily. I didn't want him coming back again tomorrow. I didn't want him coming back at all.

I didn't want to see Braden Clinton's pretty little face ever again.

But could I really turn down a sale right now? Even if it was just apple butter, what if it helped turn him around and make him into a lifelong customer?

As if that would happen from the corporate lackey who was trying to take my family's livelihood away from me.

"I told you, we're closed." I kept my eyes downcast on my work, spreading the stones smoother and smoother still.

"You're a stickler for the business hours, huh?"

I didn't say anything, afraid I might cave. Or worse, tell him off.

"Well, I suppose that's fair," he went on. "If you made the exception for me, what's stopping someone else from making the same request? Before you know it, you'd have people showing up whenever they wanted and since you live right here—" He indicated the large white house on the other side of the fence. "—it's not like you can pretend like you didn't know they were here."

"Yep. That's it." I looked him up and down. "So…goodbye."

Maybe he could leave and I could finally relax. Why did the sight of him make my heart race? Probably because he was a physical reminder of what

I was failing at.

"Okay, well, I guess I'll have to come back and try again tomorrow," he said.

Tomorrow? My plan to keep him away was blowing up in my face.

"No! Wait!" I chased him to his car, where he had already opened the door. "I can get you that apple butter. Let me just—"

Braden held up his hand. "No, no! I can't ask you to compromise your business integrity. Besides, you're losing daylight, so you better finish up."

He had a point. "But…"

"Relax, I'll come back tomorrow." He winked. "You can't get rid of me that easily." He slid into his car and started it, then immediately rolled down the window.

I walked around so I could see him better. "You're just planning on being a thorn in my side, aren't you?"

"That's the goal! You'll grow to love me."

"I doubt it. And I'm *not* going to sell, so you can forget that."

"I haven't mentioned anything about a sale today," he said. "Furthest thing from my mind."

I considered taking the rake and sliding it across his perfectly waxed car. I could almost hear the scrape of metal. "Sure, it is."

"I'll see you tomorrow." He shifted into reverse, but before he moved the car he added, "Hey, nice fence."

I glanced over at the edge of the parking lot, where I had put up a new fence using scrap wood we had in one of the old barns. It was rugged and fit the farm style of the property. It also served as a barrier, funneling people into the country store to first purchase bags before wandering around the orchard.

And now I hated it because it had been Braden's suggestion.

I looked up and saw him smirking at me as he backed out of the parking lot.

True to his word, Braden came back the next day and bought some apple butter. This time, during business hours.

I tried to hide out back, busying myself with pruning trees while noting which apple varieties were ready to be picked by the public. With the warm weather we'd been having, many of the apples were ready sooner than usual. Thankfully, the temperature was supposed to drop in another week or so, which meant that apples would ripen slower, making the harvest season last longer—and possibly

even the life of our business.

Regardless of my attempts to hide, Katie told Braden where I was. She was my newest employee, a high school student who worked part-time for minimum wage—and making a killing now that the rate was so high.

When I saw Braden walk up, I had nowhere else to hide without making it obvious that I, a grown twenty-five-year-old adult, was playing a one-sided version of hide-and-go-seek.

Instead, my strategy was to pretend like I wasn't bothered by him. I kept my eyes on my work and paid him no mind, even as I followed his approach out of the corner of my eye.

I stood at the top of a ladder with a pole pruner and trimmed off a dying branch that was taking away the energy and nutrients from the fruit-producing branches.

"Don't you have employees to do that for you?" Braden asked once he was at the bottom of the ladder.

"And shouldn't you be looking for apples in the rows marked with the green signs?" I fired back. "Those are the types of apples that are ready to be picked."

"I came to see you."

"I'm busy."

"I see that. Do you need some help?"

I finished sawing through the branch and it crashed to the ground. Satisfied, I climbed down the ladder and looked at him. He had just the faintest bits of sweat showing through his powder-blue shirt. Probably because it was sitting so tight against his thin frame. Looked like he had some muscle and—

I shook my head. Why was I looking at his body? He was the enemy.

I looked him up and down. "From you? I don't think so, pretty boy."

"You keep calling me that, I'm going to get the wrong impression."

I bent over to retrieve the branch, then dragged it down the path to the tractor I had parked at the end of the row. I hauled it up into the trailer, then wiped the sweat from my brow. "And what impression would that be?"

"That you're flirting with me."

I barked out a laugh. "Please. You're not even my type."

"Successful isn't your type?"

"*Arrogant* isn't my type. Besides, if you're trying to make any type of impression on me, showing up in your business casual is only going to make me hate you more every time I see you."

He looked down at himself. "So you're saying

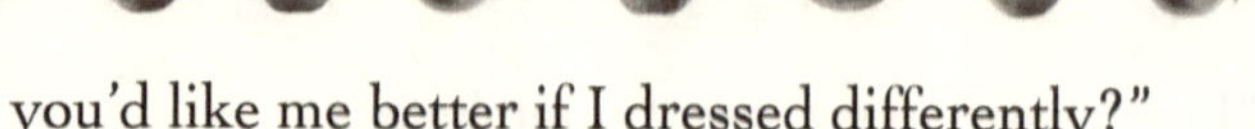

you'd like me better if I dressed differently?"

"I didn't say I'd like you at all."

"But…you kind of did. So…what? Should I wear a Chapman Farms T-shirt and jeans to impress you?"

Now it was my turn to look down at my outfit, which was exactly what he had just described. "You know, you really shouldn't be here if you're not going to buy anything."

He pulled a small empty plastic bag from behind him. Had it been tucked in his waistband? His pants were so tight he certainly couldn't have been keeping it anywhere else. "I'm about to pick some apples — when I'm in the correct spot, that is."

"Then maybe you should go."

"I'm on my way, but the orchard is huge."

"Over three hundred varieties of apples."

"And yet your parents named you after a season and *not* an apple."

I hooked an eyebrow. "Actually. I'm named after my mother's favorite apple: Autumn Glory. They're not ready to be picked yet, so if you want to come back in October you can get some then."

He scrunched his nose. "Nah. I'm in the mood for apples now. But I think I would appreciate all of these different varieties more if I didn't have to walk a mile to get to some of them."

"The apples in the crates back at the store are

from the deepest part of the orchard so you don't have to walk the whole way."

"But that kind of destroys the whole apple-picking experience."

"So what do you suggest?"

He shrugged. "A hayride taxi of some sort." He indicated the tractor. "You've got the equipment for it. Just build some benches on the back of a trailer and haul people around. It would add to the experience and it would allow people to see the whole orchard."

"And you're just offering unsolicited advice to the company you're trying to buy?"

"I like to preserve my assets."

I rolled my eyes. "If that were true, you wouldn't wear clothes so tight." I turned back to my work. "Thanks for buying the apples. You'll find some rows that are ready to be picked around the corner from here."

I climbed up the ladder and looked for more branches, doing my best to ignore him. Eventually, he took the hint and walked away.

I knew he would probably be back again, which I supposed wasn't a terrible thing. Despite it all, he had some good ideas.

"And how much would that be?" I wrote down the price on a pad of paper, knowing full well we didn't have the funds to cover our usual advertising. "Okay, well I'll talk this over with my uncles and get back to you. Thank you for taking the time to talk with me!"

I returned the phone to its cradle and leaned back in my office chair. I was at my built-in desk, which was situated in the small breezeway between the country store and the pole barn in the back.

Made up of plywood and a space heater, the office was far from luxurious, but it was the same space my father used to run the business in and I didn't want to change it at all. It was almost like the cockpit for the family business, and I was steering it right into the ground.

"Rough day?"

The voice made me jump and I spun around to see Braden poke his head into the doorway from the store.

"This area back here is only for employees." I minimized the spreadsheet on my computer that displayed our failing finances.

"Katie said it was okay."

I tried to glance around the corner, but not only was Braden blocking my way, the sound of customers in the store indicated that Katie was busy.

"I'm going to have to talk to her," I said. "What do you want?"

"Just came in to buy some of that delicious apple bread," he said.

"Then you're in the wrong place," I told him. "You should be in the store where the other customers are."

"But *am* I just another customer?" he asked.

I ignored him and turned back to the pad of paper at the desk, where I had written down different prices for different ads. If we couldn't afford advertising, then I certainly wouldn't get enough business to turn profits around.

"What are you working on?"

"Nothing that concerns you."

"I might be able to help if you trust me."

I hooked an eyebrow. "You're literally here to take my business away from me. Why would I trust you?"

"Good advice is good advice, no matter who is giving it."

I turned my chair so I was facing him. "Actually, I disagree with that. One piece of advice might be good to one person but bad to another. It depends on what your goals are."

"And your goals would be...what? Better profitability?"

I diverted my eyes, annoyed that he had pegged my needs so easily.

"That's what I thought." He indicated the desk. "Looks like you're considering some advertising options. Have you considered offering a trade?"

I had forgotten about the ad samples that lay scattered on the desk and I shifted to try to cover them. "Would you stop sticking your nose into my business?"

He shrugged. "It's something to think about. You could put up some signs around the orchard advertising different businesses in exchange for similar treatment in their business. No money exchanged, only advertising services. If you're short on cash, that's a good option and it helps build goodwill within the community."

His idea was tempting in the face of our current budget, but I was not going to give him the satisfaction of knowing that.

"Maybe you should write a book," I said. "That way your advice wouldn't be unsolicited for someone who actually wants to hear what you have to say. Assuming anyone buys the book, that is."

Braden grinned. "Maybe. But like I said, good advice is good advice." He snapped at me. "I have to get going. Gotta snag that apple bread before it's gone. Think about a trade ad."

"Goodbye!" I spun the chair around back to the desk.

"Hey, Autumn?"

Sighing, I turned my head over my shoulder. "Yes?"

"The store flows better now that you've rearranged things. Makes it easier that people can exit right into the orchard out the back door."

I was annoyed that he had pointed out that I had taken yet another one of his suggestions. I was more annoyed that he had been right.

"Goodbye!"

"See you tomorrow!"

"Please don't!" I called to him, even though I knew that he would be back.

# Chapter Eight
## AUTUMN

**W**hen I came inside, sweaty and dirty, Grandma Wanda was finishing up dinner. Salisbury steak with mashed potatoes and green beans. Despite it just being the two of us for dinner nowadays, she always made sure we had our "meat and potatoes."

Maggie barked until she saw me come through the door, then she scurried over and sniffed me for any sign of interactions with another dog. Satisfied that there were none, she turned and walked away, back to her bed in the corner.

"You go ahead and get washed up, dear," Grandma said. "This is just about done."

I stepped over to the sink and washed my hands, then

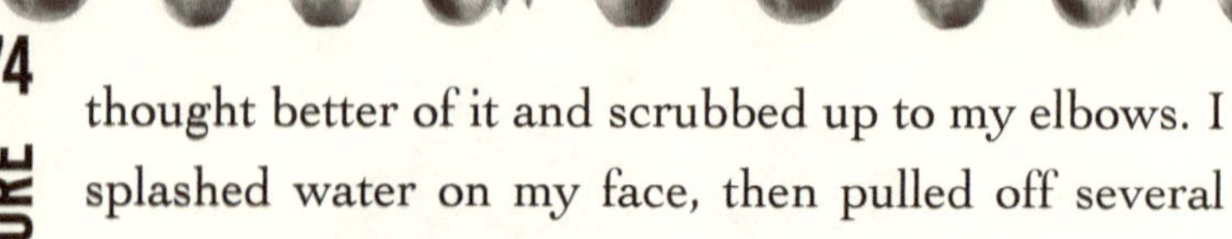



thought better of it and scrubbed up to my elbows. I splashed water on my face, then pulled off several sheets of paper towels to dry myself off.

When I saw Grandma's worried look, I said, "I'm going to take a shower after dinner, but right now I'm starving and need to eat something."

Clearly not happy with my choice, Grandma sighed. "Well, all right. Just don't make a habit of it." She dished out our plates, then carried them over to the table. "You bring over the drinks."

I filled two glasses with water and carried them over to the table.

We sat across from each other and both quietly ate our food. The thing about Grandma was that she didn't need to fill the silence with chatter. She loved talking, sure, but mostly she just loved being with her family, even if we weren't doing anything in particular.

About halfway through my plate, she finally spoke up.

"I noticed that your executive friend has been here almost every day this week."

"Braden?" I rolled my eyes to show my distaste. "He's hardly my *friend*. But yeah, he's been here a lot."

"Any more offers to buy the farm?"

"Not *officially*," I said. "But he's made it clear that

the offer is still there. As well as his intent to get me to sign all of this away."

Grandma popped another bite into her mouth. "He's cute."

"Grandma!" I nearly choked on my water, which resulted in a concerned bark from Maggie, who had transitioned to laying by Grandma's feet. "He is *not* cute!"

"Oh, don't lie. You might not like his motives but you can't deny how attractive he is."

I sat back in my seat, refusing to acknowledge or deny her statement. Sure, Braden was *traditionally* attractive, but he was certainly not *my* type of guy with his crisp ironed shirt and shiny shoes, so what did it matter? Even if I *was* interested, the fact that he wanted to *buy my family's farm* didn't lend itself to a healthy relationship. Nope. Braden Clinton was strictly off-limits.

Not that I was even interested.

Because I wasn't.

"Don't be a prude, Autumn," Grandma pushed. "If circumstances were different, he'd be turning your head just like I'm sure he does all the other girls."

I tapped my fork against my plate, refusing to say anything else.

"Admitting he's attractive isn't going to change

the way you feel about him," she added. "You can still hate him just as much whether he's the prettiest thing you've ever seen or if he grew up in Satan's trash can."

That made me smile, and softened my resolve. "Okay. Yes, he *is* cute. But I am not interested."

"That is a shame, though." Grandma turned back to her food, apparently satisfied with herself.

"What is?"

"That you're not interested in him, even a little bit—other than being attracted to him, that is."

I opened my mouth to retort, but clamped it shut and settled for a heavy sigh instead. No matter what I said, Grandma was going to believe what she wanted to believe. The annoying part was that she was usually right. Although, this time might've been different.

"All I'm saying is that if you were interested in him enough to go on a date with him, then maybe you could squeeze some more of those good ideas out of him to help turn this place around."

"His good ideas?"

"Don't pretend like I haven't noticed the way you put up that fence along the edge of the parking lot and the orchard. And I heard you telling Sammy how you wanted him to start running a hayride so people could more easily get to the trees in the back of the property, which I think is a fabulous idea."

"Grandma, Braden is the competition," I said. "He wants to *buy* our family-owned business. The one that keeps us fed and housed. The one that's supported this family for over a hundred years. You know that one?"

She waved it off. "Oh, I know that, sweetheart."

"And your pretty boy is just another cog that wants to scoop up anything with any kind of heart in it to satisfy the soulless corporation he works for!" Call me butter because I was on a roll.

Grandma shrugged. "What's the worst that can happen if you play *him* a little? Maybe he'd rub off on you and instead of the bigger guy always winning you might be able to pick his brain a little to see what other suggestions he has. I've lived long enough to know that understanding lies in the details. You're a hard worker, honey, but you are not much of a businesswoman."

I shrank back into my seat, feeling like a deflated balloon.

"That's okay!" She reached across the table for my hand. "You don't have to be the best businesswoman to ever run this place. Hell, your grandfather screwed up at least a hundred times when he was the one running the show. But you know what he learned?"

"What's that?" I picked at my food and avoided her eyes.

"That sometimes it's okay to ask for help," she said. "Especially when it's something that we don't know how to do—or don't have the time for! Think of Braden as a resource to help you make Chapman Farms a better business."

"I think you're forgetting that he's the *competition*."

She shook her head. "No, I think that's exactly the reason to ask him. Not only does he have an outsider's opinion, but he has expertise in the business."

"Does he, though? Or is he just another mindless nobody sitting in an office somewhere telling the people who are *actually* doing the work how to do their jobs?"

Grandma shrugged. "You'll never know until you talk to him. Maybe ask him to go to coffee or dinner."

I narrowed my eyes. "Do you mean a date? Grandma, I'll admit that he's cute but I hardly want to *date* him."

"There was a point in time where women didn't have very many rights in this world. Fortunately, that's no longer the case. But do you think we got those rights without emphasizing our *natural* talents—" She pushed up her boobs to further drive the point home.

I covered my face.

"No, we didn't. We had to flirt and manipulate men to a degree so they made decisions with their *downstairs* brain, if you catch my drift."

"Yeah, I got it." I was still hiding behind my face.

"The point is, you can call this *meeting* with Braden whatever you want, but you need to make sure that you meet with him on *your* terms. Otherwise, he'll always be the one in charge and, honey, you're the boss when it comes to Chapman Farms. It's time you start acting like it."

My eyes widened and I stared at her. "I *have* been acting like it!"

"Then show the cute corporate bozo just how much of a boss you are! Do what you need to do to save our family business."

I sat back in my seat. "I can't believe you're telling me to whore myself out for business."

Grandma reached for her glass. "Like I said, darling, do what you need to do. Oh, but please don't tell him I called him a bozo. I'm sure he's a very intelligent young man. I just don't want him taking our business."

I sighed as I weighed Grandma's suggestion. "You and me both."

# Chapter Nine
## BRADEN

It was after business hours at Chapman Farms by the time I made it up to Medina. The problem with staying at the hotel in Medina was that my commute to and from work went from fifteen minutes to almost an hour. That, on top of keeping up with the other aspects of my job was starting to weigh on me.

But that possible Director of Acquisitions title was calling me back to Medina to close the deal to secure it. I wanted that title if, for no other reason, than to prove that I could get it.

When I got out of the car at Chapman Farms, I saw Autumn up on a forklift, easing a large wooden crate into the center of the country store gift shop. With the two

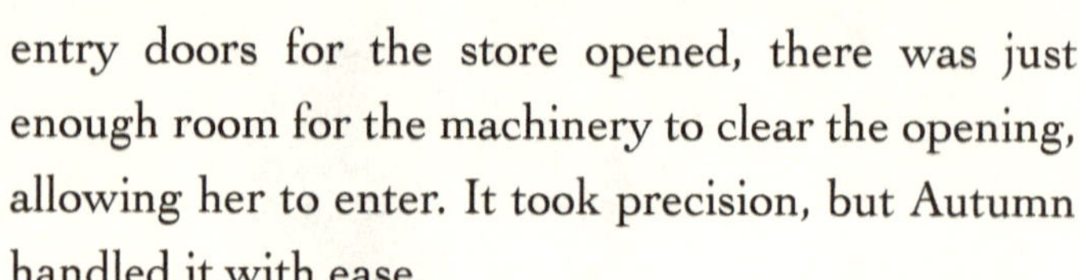



entry doors for the store opened, there was just enough room for the machinery to clear the opening, allowing her to enter. It took precision, but Autumn handled it with ease.

She waved when she saw me, then backed the forklift into its spot in the pole barn that was attached to the store through her makeshift office. Cutting the engine, she came back out and slid the barn door closed behind her.

"I wasn't sure you were going to make it out today." She closed the first door into the gift shop and waited for me to enter before she closed the second one.

"I couldn't miss annoying my favorite farmer."

Autumn rolled her eyes, and began dumping the apples from the smaller apple crates that she had stacked up on the checkout counter into the large one in the center of the room. "You mean, you couldn't miss another opportunity to give you everything my family has ever worked for."

I put up my hands in surrender. "No sales pitch today. Just wanted to make contact with you."

She studied me. "Is that some business crap you're trying on me?"

I shook my head. "No. I know none of that works on you. You're too smart."

"There you go with more crap." She dumped

more apples into the large crate in the center of the room.

"What are you doing? Isn't the point for people to go out to the orchard to pick them themselves?"

"Sure, it is. But some people physically can't do that. Or maybe they don't have the time. And then there are some varieties of apples that are too expensive or delicate to have the general public out handling them on their own, so I set up a crate in here. They still pick them themselves, like at the grocery store, but it's all in one place."

I raised my eyebrows. "Wow. I guess you're teaching me something."

"I bet that just makes you want to curl up and disappear, doesn't it?" she asked with a smirk.

I shrugged, not wanting to give her any satisfaction. "Doesn't mean that it's the best for sales."

"Maybe not, but logistically it's a move we need to make so we can cycle through as many apples as we can. If they sit on the branches too long they'll fall off or wildlife will get to them before our customers. Not to mention, my grandma will use some of these to make applesauce, baked goods, or other apple products that we'll sell in here too."

"That can't be all the apples you grow here, though," I said. "You have so many."

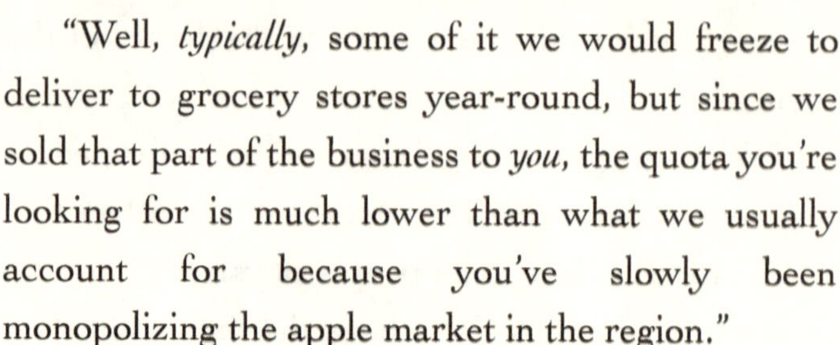



"Well, *typically*, some of it we would freeze to deliver to grocery stores year-round, but since we sold that part of the business to *you*, the quota you're looking for is much lower than what we usually account for because you've slowly been monopolizing the apple market in the region."

I eyed her. "You've been doing your research."

"You're not the only one who can do a Google search," she fired back.

"Well," I said, not sure where to go from there. "You haven't completely sold the business yet."

"Which means I have a lot of work to do." She moved around the counter and pulled out a cardboard box, which she carried over to a shelf in the corner. She moved jars of apple butter to the front and began setting the newer jars behind the older ones. "The store's closed, so you can't buy anything today. I've already settled up the cash and written the deposit slip for the bank tomorrow."

"So the U-Pick season is going well?" I asked.

She shrugged, keeping her back to me as she worked. "As well as any other year, I guess. It's steady."

I resisted the urge to tell her the mantra at Blossom Properties. *Unless you're increasing sales, you're losing business.* Steady wasn't good, at least in the eyes of our corporation.

But I kept all of that to myself. Instead, I said, "That's good."

Autumn sighed. "The truth is, without the parts of the business that we sold off, we're going to have to turn a huge profit in order to even keep the doors open, and if we keep going at the same trajectory as in years past, we're never going to get there because we don't have the income to supplement slow days for U-Pick." Her body slumped, but she kept working.

Always working.

It turned out that Autumn was a better businesswoman than either of us realized. But just because she could identify a problem, didn't mean that she could fix it.

"How do you know this year won't turn a big profit?" I remembered how Sara used to hate it when I would "fix" things. Women liked to just vent sometimes, but I wasn't sure if that's all that Autumn was doing so I treaded carefully. "It's still early."

"True, it's only the second weekend into September," she admitted. "But unless I get a big surge of customers that stays until the end of the season—and then comes back again year-after-year, I don't think we're going to make it."

I let out a breath that I'd been holding, trying to keep my professional composure as she unloaded her

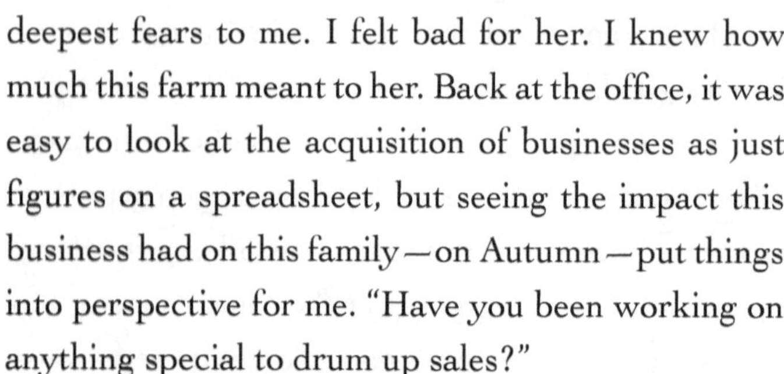

deepest fears to me. I felt bad for her. I knew how much this farm meant to her. Back at the office, it was easy to look at the acquisition of businesses as just figures on a spreadsheet, but seeing the impact this business had on this family—on Autumn—put things into perspective for me. "Have you been working on anything special to drum up sales?"

Finished stocking, she tossed the empty box by the door, then crossed the room to grab another one behind the counter. "I've been trying to coordinate with more local businesses to sell some of our products in-store, which I'm hoping will help. But that stuff could also just sit on a shelf."

"Have you thought about maybe going and selling stuff in person?" I suggested. "I know you're a regular at farmer's markets, but maybe you'd stand out more at another local business."

She shook her head. "I don't have the manpower for that kind of thing, and I don't have the time in my day to do it myself." Reaching back, she gathered her hair up and, with a few casual gestures, pulled the hair tie from her wrist and piled her brown hair up on the top of her head. "I'm just afraid that this is all too little too late." She turned and seemed to notice me for the first time. "Of course, I'm not sure why I'm even telling you all of this. I'm sure you're just eating all of this up to report back to your bosses as proof that Chapman Farms will be another orchard to add to your roster."

"Not at all." I bit my bottom lip. That wasn't necessarily true. I wasn't going to immediately report back to Mr. Ramsey, but if he asked how things were going I would have to tell him the truth. After all, I worked for Blossom Properties, not Chapman Farms.

But my success at Blossom Properties would mean the end of Chapman Farms. The end of Autumn's livelihood — of her home. That messed with my head.

"Can I offer a suggestion?" I started.

She turned and crossed her arms. "Haven't you already made one?"

"Okay, *another* one then."

She raised her eyebrows, giving permission to continue.

"Maybe you can work that in to your week. Like, coordinate with different businesses around town and put together a map and do a little pop-up shop at different locations — then maybe put together a scavenger hunt, of sorts. If someone stops and visits you at all locations, maybe they get a free bag of apples or something."

Autumn shook her head, causing some of her hair to fall out of the messy bun on top of her head. "No,

I don't have the manpower for that. I told you that." She moved behind the counter again and started piling up empty boxes onto the counter.

"So you can do it yourself."

"I have too many other things to do."

"So maybe close the store for a day each week — like a Monday — or maybe a Thursday — and do the pop-up shop thing then, instead of running the orchard."

Autumn tossed her head back and barked out a single laugh. "Ha! You think the way to *save* the farm is to close it more often?" She pulled a box cutter out of a drawer behind the counter and began breaking down the boxes.

I shrugged. "I don't know. I just think that you're kind of out of sight, out of mind, since you're not exactly *in* town."

She looked up at me and shot daggers with her eyes. "I have to be! How do you expect a farm to fit in —"

"I know, I know." I put out my hands to ward off any further defense. "I'm just pointing out that it might be a disadvantage to you."

"Yeah, well, short of me restarting the farm somewhere closer to town — which isn't going to happen for many reasons — I'm stuck." She busied herself straightening displays on the checkout counter.

My heart went out to her. Sure, I was supposed to be buying up her business, but she was making an honest effort, putting in the work…and still failing. And all because of the circumstances that she had inherited.

"Okay, so if you can't go out to different businesses in town, then maybe bring them to you?" I suggested.

"Like what?" Autumn resumed breaking down the boxes.

"Maybe have businesses set up booths here in the gift shop—or maybe have them set up in the orchard, maybe down that main path leading to all the different kinds of apples? Or maybe you can reach out and get crafters or some other people to help draw a crowd. Not only would the vendors pay their fees, but you'd bring in more people who would buy apples and all of your other products too."

Autumn was shaking her head before I finished. "I just told you, I don't have the manpower to devote to something like that. And I don't have the time to do it myself."

"So I'll do it." The words left my mouth before I realized exactly what I was committing myself to.

But she picked up on it. "You will?"

Seeing the hint of a smile grace the corners of her mouth convinced me that this was something I *had* to

do, regardless of the consequences.

But I couldn't lose my job in the process.

I cleared my throat and looked away. "Yeah, well, you know…um, a healthy business is an attractive business for Blossom Properties to snatch up and we want to make sure we're not just taking in a business just to liquidate assets and readjust funds to other parts of our corporation. We want to take in a business with a strong following, and this would help strengthen your following for when you sell it to us."

Autumn's face dropped. "Oh. I see." She studied me further, and even though I examined all the suggested impulse purchases along the checkout counter, I could feel her eyes on me. "Well, who knows? Maybe this will save Chapman Farms after all and we won't be accepting your offer to buy. You have a deal."

My head snapped in her direction. "We do?"

"For you to help put together this vendor show," she said. "Not for you to buy the farm."

I blinked, still surprised that she had agreed to it after that spiel of bullshit I had just given her. "Okay. But, if I'm going to work for you, it needs to be undercover."

"Oh, you won't be working," she clarified. "You're *volunteering*, remember?"

She really was a good businesswoman. Always

watching the bottom line and calling in favors.

"Regardless," I pushed. "We can't let word spread that I'm helping. I would lose my job."

"That's going to be hard to do when you're making phone calls to businesses all over town."

I thought about that. "Then maybe I give them a fake name."

She rolled her eyes. "Okay, double-oh-seven. You do that."

"But if I'm going to call up businesses that you have connections with, then I need to make those connections with you," I said.

"What do you mean?"

"I've seen most of the operations up here—"

"That's what happens when you show up every day and force yourself into my business."

"—and I need to see your connections *outside* of this place," I went on. "The people you work with. Your regular customers. People who might have something to offer in the way of help for this vendor show. I might be staying here in town, but this is *your* hometown."

She seemed surprised at that. "You're staying here in town?"

"Yeah, at that little hotel on West Center Street. It's small, but it's nice."

"Don't you work out in Buffalo?"

I nodded. "Cheektowaga, but close enough."

She looked me over. "And you've been going back and forth to work?"

I looked down at myself and the outfit I'd chosen for the day. Business casual, leaning more on the business side. More blue—why did I pack so many blue shirts? "It's kind of a requirement of the job."

"So you've been driving from Medina to Cheektowaga every day, just so you can stay close to me?" Her eyes grew wide and she quickly recovered. "Close to Chapman Farms, that is."

I shrugged. "Well, yeah. This is a big deal for me and my career, so some sacrifices had to be made. Besides, it's not like I have anyone waiting for me at home, so I can afford to take the time to live remotely for a little bit."

"Huh." She crossed her arms and considered that.

"Is that okay?"

"I mean, yeah. It is. I'm just…surprised, I guess."

I wasn't sure what she was surprised about, exactly, but I also didn't care to be analyzed anymore than I already had. "Anyway, I know you have connections to businesses in town and I want to see more of how that works so I can finagle some of those connections to work out for the show."

She chewed on her bottom lip. "I don't know how

I feel about introducing my competition to my business partners and friends in town. I don't want it to seem like I'm endorsing you if you come and take over the business down the line without my consent."

"I can't take your business without your consent," I clarified. "Besides, I promise I won't use these connections against you. Honestly, I'm just the deal closer. If Blossom were to acquire Chapman, someone else would be in the driver's seat when it came time to merging your business into ours. So really, you have nothing to lose and potentially a lot to gain."

Autumn let out a heavy sigh. "Fine. Monday morning we can get coffee at the shop on East Center Street. Shouldn't be too far of a walk from where you're staying. Let's say, nine o'clock, so that gives me enough time to get the store open and things settled here before I waste my time with you."

Nine o'clock. I had another meeting Monday morning at nine.

"Is that okay?" she pushed, recognizing my hesitation.

I nodded. "Sure. I'll make it work."

"Glad you could squeeze me into your busy schedule."

"I'd squeeze you in anywhere."

She looked at me, disgusted. "Gross."

# Chapter Ten
## AUTUMN

I saw Braden crossing Main Street as I turned onto East Center Street. By the time I parked the car in front of the coffee shop, he was standing right outside the door.

"Look at that," he said. "Perfect timing!"

I closed the door to my truck and went around to the back. "Look at that! You found it!"

"It was a long walk from way over there." He pointed across Main Street, where his hotel was.

I pulled another crate out of the back and waited as Braden held the door open for me to step inside.

"Hey Autumn! Got another delivery for us?" Hattie wiped down the counters with a rag, but tossed it over her shoulder when we walked in.

I set the heavy crate down on the floor beside the dessert display. "Yep. I have apple scones, a few more apple pies, and some apple cider donuts."

"Oooh, those sell quick!" Hattie said. She noticed Braden lingering behind me and turned her attention to him. "Are you ready to order, sir?"

"He's, uh…he's actually with me." I cleared my throat. "Not *with* me, but we came here together—or we met each other here." I clamped my mouth shut to stop the rush of word vomit. After I took a moment to recuperate, I introduced him. "This is Braden. He's from Blossom Properties." I eyed Hattie carefully, trying to convey a message without so many words. "Braden, this is Hattie. She helped open Medina's very own local coffee shop."

Braden reached across the dessert display. "Pleased to meet you. I'm just being Autumn's shadow today, meeting some of her contacts. How long have you been supporting Chapman Farms?"

"Actually, it was Autumn who first reached out to me," Hattie clarified. "When we first opened, she wanted to support another local business by doing a little bit more than just buying a cup of coffee— which, of course, she also does every time she's here."

"Speaking of, I'll take a mocha latte, please," I added quickly.

"And what'll you have?" she asked Braden.

He looked up at the large menu hanging on the wall toward the ceiling. "Um…I'll take an Americano."

"Excellent choice." Hattie moved down the counter to begin preparing our drinks.

"So Autumn reached out to you and now you're business partners?" he asked.

"Not exactly," Hattie said. "We're more like another outlet in town for Chapman Farms to sell their goods at—at least, the ones that don't grow on trees."

The bell above the door rang as a line of people stepped in. Gently, I pressed my hand against Braden's arm to signal that he should move down the counter even further. With the way the old building was and where the counter was placed, there was only a small awkward waiting area for drinks.

After another few minutes, Hattie set our drinks on the counter and quickly cashed us out—Braden tried to pay for mine, but I swiped my card before he was able to. Once we had our drinks, I ushered Braden over to the small sitting area in another room.

Years ago, the sitting area space was a separate storefront, but it was so small that it was eventually merged with the neighboring one. One of the previous owners had put in a beautiful brick fireplace

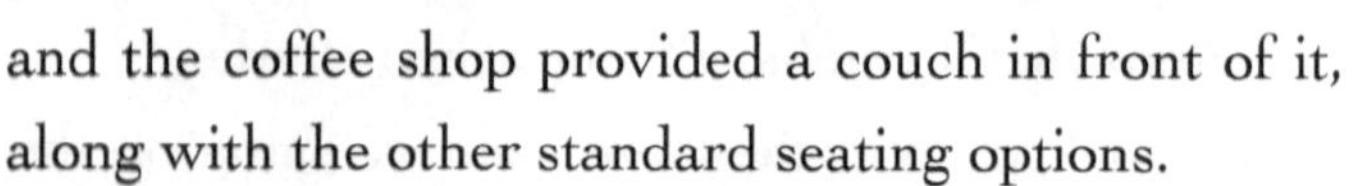

and the coffee shop provided a couch in front of it, along with the other standard seating options.

We took our seats at opposite ends of the couch. My hope was that it would provide me enough cover so that anyone stopping in for a cup of coffee would hopefully miss seeing me with my back turned to them. But luck hadn't been on my side lately.

The line of customers that came in after us quickly filtered out. The Monday morning rush meant more people coming and going than ordering and staying, which gave me and Braden a decent amount of privacy.

"Well, it sounds like you're a good person." Braden realized halfway through the sip of his coffee what he had implied. He choked a little as he rushed to spit out an amendment to his statement, which, in effect made him dribble coffee down his chin. "Not that I needed anymore proof of that. I knew you were a good person before. It's just…this was a nice reminder. Another example. You're perfect—I mean, you—"

I put up my hand up to save him any additional embarrassment. "I got what you meant. And I appreciate you saying that. But it's not me. The truth is that Medina is a place where people want to come and explore and, in your case, stay here, and that's because of the tight-knit business community supporting each other."

Braden nodded. "A rising tide lifts all boats."

"Which is not something you get with corporate commercialism," I said.

"Fair point."

"As you made it abundantly clear, Chapman Farms is just outside of town, so if I want to be a part of the tight-knit community, I need to maintain these connections that evolved naturally."

He nodded. "Which is why I think some kind of festival or vendor show would be a good idea. It's a way to solidify your family's orchard as a staple in Medina."

I eyed him. I still didn't understand why he was helping me, or the business. Sure, it made sense that the work he did now to build up Chapman Farms would serve Blossom Properties well if they eventually bought us out, but I wasn't convinced that was really his motivation. I was suspicious—and guarded—and I didn't want to let him get closer to my family's business than I already had.

"I don't think it'll work," I said.

He shifted so he was facing me across the couch. The leg of his black pants pulled higher, revealing gray argyle socks underneath. A crack in his armor revealing itself. "How could it not! It'll draw people in, give you an excuse to advertise without delivering a sales pitch, and if you do it well, its success will build year-after-year."

I sipped my coffee before I laid it all out for him. "Here's my reality: we're already a couple weeks in to this apple season and now all of a sudden you've gotten an idea for a festival that you seem to think we can pull off. Meanwhile, I still have to keep the farm running on a shoestring budget, maintain the shop, and put up with you."

He smirked at that.

"Besides, my uncles have equal ownership of the farm, even though they don't work on the day-to-day stuff. They want to sell and get it off their hands while we still can. So they've given me the deadline to turn the finances around by the end of *this* apple season. That's early November. So unless your festival is a huge moneymaker, I'm not relying on this year-to-year success because *my* reality is that I'll be the failure that lost my family's four-generations-long business and I'll be left working a soul-sucking job by this time next year."

Braden sipped his coffee, allowing only his eyebrows to raise as I drove each point home. "Are you done?"

I rolled my eyes. Typical man. He wasn't even listening and dismissed my problems to something trivial. I let out a heavy sigh and wrapped my hands around my cup. "Yes, I suppose so."

"Can I ask questions now?"

I shrugged an acknowledgment.

"When does Chapman Farms usually see the final big rush for U-Pick? Like, when do you usually see the biggest rush of customers?"

I rocked my head back and forth. "Depends on the weather."

"Give it your best guess based on historic data. Assume the weather will be perfect."

"The weather is *never* perfect because it's never the same year-to-year, especially lately."

"Come on!" he urged. "Work with me here."

I let out another sigh. Why did I agree to coffee? Oh yeah, Grandma Wanda wanted to pimp me out to pick his brain for ideas to save the farm. This was one of his ideas, so I needed to roll with it. "Probably the middle of October. Although we get people into the beginning of November, but that—"

"Depends on the weather," he finished with a nod. "Got it. I think we can pull it off."

I laughed. "You're crazy."

"I'm envisioning it being called the Apple Festival at Chapman Farms—probably shortened to Apple Fest. It'll be a way to celebrate the apple harvest season, bringing in members of this tight-knit

community you're a part of, but bringing them to *you*." He pointed at me to drive the point home. "They could each set up to sell something, but most of the people should be driven through your shop in order to increase your sales. Make the whole show an experience for everyone involved, which will make them *want* to come year after year." He stopped when he saw the blank look on my face. "I take it you don't like any of this?"

"No, it's not that. It's just that, realistically, there's no way we can pull any of this off in a few weeks. I mean, we're almost in the middle of September already, so we're talking about getting this pulled off in five weeks, to turn a big enough profit by the beginning of November." I shook my head. "It's just not going to happen. And even if you *could*, somehow, do it, what happens if it rains? What happens if nobody shows up? What happens if we run out of apples before then?"

"Do you have a barn you could clear out in case of rain?"

"Well, yeah. I guess so. But—"

"So leave the rest to me," he said.

I ran my finger over the rim of the coffee lid. "Anything like this would need to be run by my uncles first, since they're equal partners in this business. Especially if it means spending any money on this."

Braden nodded. "Okay. I'll draft up a plan, then."

I couldn't help but smirk. It was nice to have some sense of direction with the business in the midst of all the drowning I had been doing.

"What?" he asked as my smile widened.

I averted my eyes down, studying my coffee cup, which was a little less than halfway empty at that point. "Nothing."

"No, what?" he pushed.

"You've just been helping me, which I appreciate, but…" I trailed off and shook my head.

"But…?" He leaned down to catch my eye as he pushed the question.

I took a deep breath. "I just have to keep reminding myself that you're the competition. Why are you helping me, again?"

He shrugged and looked away. "I don't know. It just…seems like the right thing to do."

"Even though it's going against what you originally came to Medina to do?"

"I haven't worked through all of that yet."

We fell silent. I didn't want to push him further in case he decided to change his mind. I was doubtful that this festival would turn things around, but at the moment I didn't have any other ideas of how to bring in any extra revenue.

"Do you actually like your job?" I asked.

"I'm good at it."

"That wasn't the question."

Braden seemed to consider that as he fell silent again.

"I didn't think it was a hard question," I said. "You either like it or you don't."

He chuckled once to himself and smiled. "It's a little more complicated than that."

"In what way?"

He cleared his throat and met my eyes. "I first took the job to pay for my wife's medical bills."

My eyes darted down to his left hand, which was empty, then back up at him. "You're married?"

"No," he said quickly. "Not anymore."

I remained quiet as what he wasn't saying sunk into my consciousness. "What did she have?"

"She died from complications related to her diabetes," he said. "Her kidneys failed, which we had been expecting, but then she could never get high enough on the transplant list to get one. She was on dialysis, which took a pretty big toll on her body. Our sister-in-law—her brother's wife—used to take her to dialysis appointments, but the one day she went to pick her up, she found Sara sitting on the couch under a blanket." He cleared his throat again, which had been growing thicker the more he talked. "She was gone. Like she had taken a nap and never woke up. The doctors think it was a brain aneurysm, which was probably caused from the frequent pokes in her arm from the dialysis. She was twenty-four."

I wiped at the tears prickling my eyes. "Oh, Braden…" Before I realized what I was doing, I reached across the couch and took his hand. It wasn't until our skin made contact that I understood the significance of what I'd just done.

But he squeezed my hand back, so I left it there.

He nodded. "It's okay. It was about a year and a half ago, so things have gotten…" He shook his head. "I can't say it's gotten any easier, but I've adjusted to my new life, I guess. The hardest part was the lost potential, you know? Like, everything we had planned was suddenly impossible. We dated through high school. Married right after college. We had planned on starting a family, but then when things took a turn for the worse with her health and…" He trailed off again. "So yeah. That's my sob story."

I gave his hand another squeeze. "I'm so sorry, Braden. That's awful."

"Thanks. After Sara passed, I buried myself in my work to keep my mind off things. I never thought I'd still be working at a place like Blossom almost two years after I first started."

My heart was racing and I wasn't sure why. I knew it took a lot for him to tell me everything he had and I wanted to tread carefully. "Well, I might not have known you through high school, and I don't really know you now, but from what I've seen so far, you seem to be a good person at heart too. And I think that matters more than who is paying your salary."

He smiled at me and squeezed my hand back. For a moment, sipping coffee in front of the fire, we were the only two people in the world.

# Chapter Eleven
## AUTUMN

**M**y body was exhausted, but the work wasn't completely done yet. I had spent all day sweating in the sun but, true to typical September evenings, once the sun had set, the fall chill kicked in, leaving me shivering.

I pulled on a hoodie, grabbed two thermoses and began filling them with warm apple cider.

"Expecting someone?" Grandma Wanda's voice surprised me as she came into the kitchen from behind.

"Nope."

"I noticed you pulled two lawn chairs outside too."

"I'm going to use one as a footstool," I told her. "I have some brush to burn and I'm going to sit out by the

fire to make sure it doesn't catch on that old barn —or worse, the house. The last thing this place needs is a house fire."

"Decided to take my advice?" It was evident on Grandma's face that she wasn't buying a word I was saying.

"What advice?" I played dumb.

She nodded. "Mm-hmm. Will you be in for dinner, or should I eat without you?"

"Um…" I looked outside and eyed up the pile I had spent the day dragging to the fire pit. "You can probably eat without me. That stuff is pretty green still and will probably take a while to burn." I started to the door with both thermoses in my arms. "You don't need to wait up for me either."

"Okay." The smile was evident in her voice. "Have fun on your date."

"It's not a date!" I hollered back into the house, but Grandma ignored me.

Outside, I set my drinks next to the one lawn chair and used the lighter in my pocket to start up some of the dried leaves. The flame caught on, and I used my hand to shield the wind from putting out the delicate flame. As the fire grew, I added more dried leaves, then larger sticks before eventually adding larger branches to it. Within twenty-five minutes, I had a roaring fire and the gentle breeze carried the

smoke down toward the orchard, away from the house and, most importantly, me.

True to my word, I held the insulated mug of warm apple cider close to me as I put up my feet on the other lawn chair. I pulled out my phone and began to read the romance book I had been trying to get into all summer. Now was the perfect time to really dive in.

Except, as hard as I tried, I couldn't help but keep stealing glances from down the driveway. Braden hadn't been back to Medina since we met for coffee on Monday. Did I scare him off? Did I care? Was I finally free of him? Is that what I wanted?

I shook my head and turned my attention back to my book, but my thoughts kept drifting to Braden. Would he enjoy sitting out by a fire? Or would he complain about the cold and the smoke and just want to go inside? I thought he might like it. Apparently there was more to him underneath those tight dress shirts he always wore.

Not that I ever thought about him in that way.

Giving up on my book, I crouched down by the fire and added another branch, sending embers and smoke up into the air. The fire burned brighter as new leaves caught. I settled back in my chair and admired my work.

Unnatural light illuminated the night air from

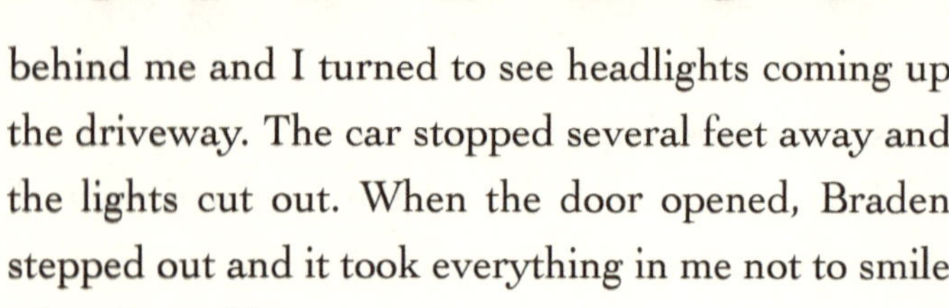

behind me and I turned to see headlights coming up the driveway. The car stopped several feet away and the lights cut out. When the door opened, Braden stepped out and it took everything in me not to smile when I saw him.

What the hell was wrong with me? One little hand hold and I was swooning over this man. I needed to get a grip.

"Sorry I'm late," he said.

"Late?" I asked. "What do you mean?"

"I've been swamped at work since I've been spending so much time up here, and with the commute to Medina, by the time I get up here it's pretty late and I don't want to bother you because I know you get up early and —"

I held up my hand to stop him. "Please. I wasn't waiting for you."

He looked down at the second lawn chair and second thermos. "You weren't?"

"The chair was for my feet. And I really like apple cider."

Skepticism showed on his face. "Sure. Well, would you mind it, then, if I take over your footstool?"

I pulled my feet away and waved toward the chair, but looked away to feign disinterest. "If you insist."

Braden readjusted the second chair so it was side-by-side with mine and settled in. He grabbed the second thermos and sipped from it. "Wow! This is great! I haven't had apple cider in years."

"*Years*? What's stopping you? Are you allergic to taste as much as you are to style?"

He looked down at his shirt—another powder-blue dress shirt—how many of them did he have? I had to admit, he did look sharp. But did he really need to wear the same thing every day?

"Says the one who is checking me out," he fired back.

I pointed. "Your nipples are showing."

He looked down and covered them. "Is that something you like?"

"Is that shirt a child's small?"

"Did you pull that sweatshirt out of your dad's closet?"

At that, I lost all interest in our banter. I turned back to look at the fire.

"Sorry," he said. "I don't know what I said, but I obviously hit a nerve. That wasn't—you're not—"

"It's fine." I just wanted him to shut up.

We were quiet as we watched the fire burn. It crackled and popped, and I studied it as it slowly consumed the branches, turning them into ash and smoke.

"This is really beautiful." Braden cut into my thoughts.

I glanced over at him to see what exactly he was referring to, and followed his gaze to our old barn sitting adjacent to our house. It was large and red, although a lot of the paint had been chipping away for years. The warm glow from the fire illuminated the side, revealing the large banner that had been painted on it years ago by my grandfather that read, *Chapman Farms Family Orchards* in big artistic block letters. Like the rest of the barn, that signage badly needed a touch-up as well.

"The barn? It's been here every time you visited."

"Not just the barn." He curled in on himself, rubbing his arms up and down. "Everything. The fire. The orchard in the background. The barn. The moon. All of it."

"Don't get stuff like this in the city, do you?"

"Not to this extent," he admitted. "What do you even use that barn for? I've been showing up basically every day for two weeks and the most I've seen you use it is to store your tractors."

"That's about all that's in there," I said. "Although it used to be the main barn for the orchard." I gestured to the sign that had slowly been chipping away. "It was the icon of our business for a while."

"It's not anymore?"

I shook my head. "With modernized equipment that needed to be held in more temperature-controlled rooms, and with more stringent health department rules, we needed to build another one, which is the one that's attached to the gift shop." I pointed to the pole barn that sat adjacent to the old barn so he knew which one I was talking about.

"So it's just been sitting empty?"

"Not *empty*. You said it yourself, we store things in there."

He rolled his eyes. "Okay, so it's a garage. That's it?" He scooted his chair closer to the fire and took another sip of his drink.

I followed suit so we were more in line with one another. The heat from the fire licked against my front while my back was getting chillier. But I was still enjoying the conversation.

"I have this idea that it could be turned into a hotel or something cool," I admitted. "Maybe not a full hotel, more like an Airbnb-type thing. I love the idea of repurposing old barns into living spaces. I've just been too busy keeping up with the orchard. And then there's the cost and everything and…it's just not going to happen."

Braden glanced over at the house. Light only glowed through a few of the windows, which I knew to be the kitchen and living room. I was grateful that

I didn't see Grandma Wanda's head in one of them.

"Your house is pretty big," he said. "Is it just you and your grandmother who live here?"

I nodded. "Yeah."

"Surely you can't be using the whole thing."

"No, actually most of it is empty, unfortunately. There's a whole separate wing that's sitting unused."

"Really?" he asked. "Why did you build it so big, then?"

"It wasn't always," I told him. "I'm diving into a bit of a family history lesson here, but I'll try to keep it brief. Basically, when my family first came to the US in the late 1800s, they started this orchard and built the house on the property to live in it. But then they had kids and they needed to work on the farm to keep it going, so they added on to the house over and over again. At one point, there were four generations living in this house, although you can hardly count me at the time because I was just a baby when my great-grandparents passed away."

"So your family's *always* lived here."

I nodded. "Up until my Uncle Stan and Uncle Jim both got married and moved into their own places. Actually, I think my dad was born in this house, but that might just be a family rumor. My grandma likes to tell stories."

Braden smiled. "This place really means a lot to you."

I shrugged. "It's my family's history. It's what supported them when they first moved here, and it's been supporting us ever since. I don't want to be the one who ends all of that." I looked down at my thermos. The apple cider was almost gone, and what was left of it had gone cold. "Too bad that's probably exactly what's going to happen. And good luck selling this massive house. Not only is it so big and unnecessary in this day and age, but I've been neglecting it to focus on the farm. Not to mention, my grandma would chain herself to the stair banister if anyone ever tried to get her to leave."

He laughed. "Well, as amusing as *that* would be, I think you're doing a better job keeping things going than you realize. I just think there's untapped potential here that you can't even see because you're too close to it."

I gave him a skeptical look. "Like what?"

"Well, for starters, I think the house would make a much better inn than the barn. Get it designated as a historical landmark and there would be some tax credits involved, which would help your bottom line. Not to mention, if it's been added onto, then there's gotta be a logical place inside to seal off the private

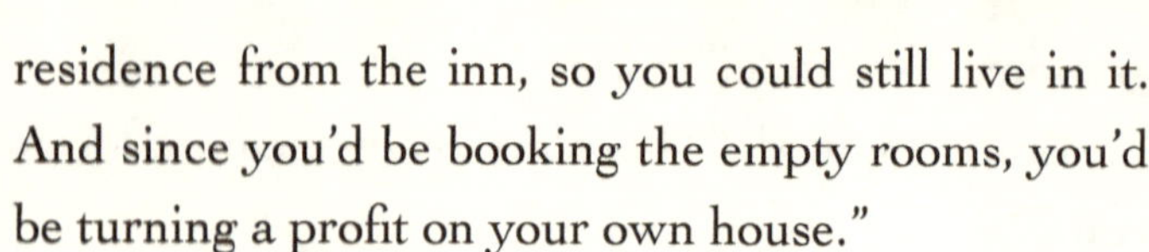

residence from the inn, so you could still live in it. And since you'd be booking the empty rooms, you'd be turning a profit on your own house."

"Huh. I guess I never thought about that. But is there really enough demand for an inn outside of town? I mean, the center of town only has two hotels and, like you've seen yourself, the one is pretty small."

"True," he said. "But you have something the center of town doesn't: an event venue right outside your door." He gestured to the barn.

"An event center? What do you mean?"

"You could put a full-sized kitchen on the lower level, full dining area on the upper level. Book up a wedding, offer an attractive rate to your inn for the wedding party, and you'd be booking both the inn and the event venue for every wedding. Even if your wedding season is only during the summer, you'd be making bank before the apple season even hit. And if this Apple Fest idea takes off like I think it will, you could use the barn as a backup in case of rain — or extra vendor space."

I still wasn't buying into it. I couldn't. There had been too many other ideas thrown around that never took off because when push came to shove, we just couldn't afford it. Not while trying to protect our core business, which had always been —

and would always be—apples.

"That all sounds nice," I said, "but how are we supposed to pay for it when we're struggling to pay the bills we have now?"

"You own the property outright, correct?"

I nodded.

"So apply for a home equity loan," he said. "With the size of the property and the number of buildings on it, I would assume it'd be worth quite a bit, which is all money you'd be able to spend on these new ventures. Of course, you don't want to spend *all* of it, just in case something happens, but it'll give you the wiggle room you're looking for to make these changes."

I stared at the fire, letting him talk. It was nice to dream, but I was afraid to let hope creep into those dreams.

"*And*," he went on, "you would probably want to do the project in phases. I would say probably the barn first, so you can start booking events and then once you've established yourself in that market, you can add in the renovations to the house and finish the inn part, which would add to not only the events part of your business, but would encourage people from a wider geographic range to come and stay to visit the orchard for the apples. Plus, the income from booking weddings would help pay for the inn project

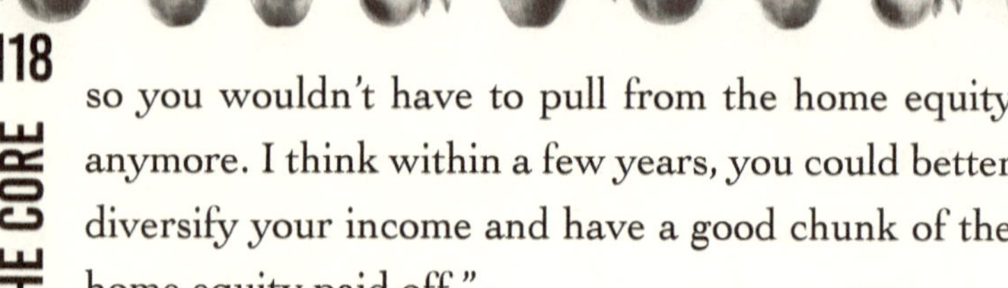



so you wouldn't have to pull from the home equity anymore. I think within a few years, you could better diversify your income and have a good chunk of the home equity paid off."

"And what if this fails? What if we take the loan, spend the money, and nobody shows up?" I couldn't help but consider the worst-case scenario. "That would put us in such a financial hole that we wouldn't be able to recover from."

"What's the alternative to *not* doing this?" he asked. "You sell the business—and the property—to a place like Blossom Properties, which means you'll lose everything anyway. What's the bigger risk? Giving up, or putting up a fight and trying to make it work yourself?"

I sighed and turned back to the fire. I hated how he just dismissed my concerns. What was worse was that I hated how he made it all sound so *easy*. Like it was the most natural thing in the world to do. Only an idiot wouldn't think of it.

Someone like me.

"You just have it all figured out, don't you?"

He shrugged and leaned back further in his chair, although he didn't quite look relaxed. His shoulders were raised as he tucked his arms in close to himself with the chill. "It's what I do."

I considered offering to go in and get him a

sweatshirt, but then I remembered the jab he made about my own sweatshirt and decided to let him suffer a little. He'd live.

"You're really good at this stuff," I admitted.

Braden eyed me. "But…"

"But nothing."

"Really? There's no insult attached to that? You don't think it's a shame I use my expertise at a place like Blossom Properties?"

I rocked my head back and forth. "Well, I don't think that's necessarily a *good* thing, but I can see why they hired you. Why they like you. If you ever get tired of crushing small businesses to make you rich, I might even consider hiring you here. Of course, you'd have to take a serious pay cut."

He smiled, but didn't take the bait.

"So anyway," I went on in his silence, "um…how does one get *into* business?"

"What do you mean?"

"Well, you seem to know a lot about this stuff. I was just wondering how you got to be so well-versed in all of this financial mumbo-jumbo."

He laughed. "Are you checking my credentials? Is this an informal interview?"

I rolled my eyes and shifted so my body was turned away from him. "Never mind."

"Well *boss*, I have a degree in business from UB,

which I thought would make me more marketable to employers, but I didn't have any consistent internship work experience in any one line of business, so nobody really knew what to do with me. I took a scattershot approach to internships to see what I would like and apparently that hurt me in the long run. But I did get an interview with this small non-profit that eventually hired me. They provided additional literacy support for all kinds of people. They helped develop reading skills for special needs adults or people just learning English as a new language. They did some tutoring for students who needed extra help, and they also provided free books to families that didn't have access to books."

I was pleasantly surprised that despite my initial reactions, Braden actually *did* have a heart at one point. And a moral compass. "Sounds like a noble job. I didn't realize you were so into reading."

He shrugged. "I mean, I like reading, but my job there wasn't actually helping the people in that kind of direct way. I was the one who scoured the internet for grants and filled out the applications and helped allocate the money. I worked on a lot of fundraising projects, one of which was a huge one that brought in ten thousand dollars to the non-profit and got us a lot of press, which sparked the interest of my boss at Blossom Properties."

"And that's when you decided to sell your soul and move into the corporate world?"

"Actually, no, it was when my wife got sick and I needed to find a job with a good health insurance plan to support her that I decided to find work elsewhere."

"Oh." I felt about six inches tall for the jab I had just made. "How long were you two married?"

"A little more than three years. We dated through high school, got married at twenty. Actually, we lived with her brother Lenny and his wife for a bit while we finished college, then we moved into an apartment together. We thought it would just be a starter place until we could buy our own house, but then she got sick and…" He cleared his throat and sat up straighter in his chair. "Anyway, here I am, years later, still living in that same apartment."

"I'm sorry."

"It's okay. Life happens. Even though I can afford to find something else—hell, I can even afford to buy that house we had dreamed about—I can't bring myself to leave the place that she was so proud of. We both were. It was our first home." He shook his head. "That probably sounds stupid."

"No, I get it," I said. "That's one of the reasons I'm so attached to this place. This is my home. It's

where I have so many memories of my family, but especially my parents."

"They're not with you anymore?" he asked gently.

I shook my head. "They were killed in a car crash last year. They were making deliveries to a grocery store. My Uncle Jim usually made the deliveries with my dad, but he was sick and couldn't do it. My mom didn't like the idea of my dad driving that truck by himself, so she went along with him. If Uncle Jim hadn't stayed home…" I shook my head to clear that train of thought. It wasn't helping anybody. "Anyway, a car cut in front of them and my dad lost control of the truck. They were thrown from the vehicle. The EMTs said they died immediately." I shook my head, fighting back the tears. "Their deaths put me as an equal partner with my uncles in the business. And, I believe, it was one of the major reasons why my Uncle Jim wanted to sell the wholesale part of the business. I don't think he ever wanted to get back into a truck that had taken my parents. He was too racked with guilt."

"I can imagine," he said. "And I'm sorry about making that crack about your sweatshirt."

I had momentarily forgotten about it, but his reminder brought those same discomforting feelings back. I shifted in my seat.

Braden reached over and took my hand. His was freezing, but I didn't dare draw attention to it. Even his icy hand was a comfort. It was a reminder that I wasn't alone. I had so few of those anymore.

"Anyway, that's really the reason why I'm holding on to this farm so much. Why I'm desperate to see it succeed. I want to honor my parents—and my family's legacy. I want to make them happy, even if they're not with me anymore."

"For what it's worth, I think you're doing a fine job running the farm."

I scoffed and pulled my hand away from his. "Please. I don't need your pity."

He sat up in his chair and leaned closer in my direction. "I mean it."

"No offense, but you don't know what you're talking about. The finances are in the toilet. In the last two years we've sold off two-thirds of the business just to keep the orchard alive, and we're *one* season away from shutting down for good." I gestured to the barn and the house. "All those dreams we had just talked about are just that—dreams."

"I told you I'd help you."

I rolled my eyes again. "You'd get fired if you helped the business you're supposed to be buying. If we turned things around, we'd have even more reason to turn down your offer."

"I already worked on a marketing plan for the Apple Fest," he pressed on. "I've already put out some feelers into the Buffalo community to see if anyone would be interested in being a vendor. I'm counting on getting a lot of buy-in from Medina businesses too."

I turned to face him, feeling my resolve soften. Had he really put in work on his own time for our farm? Is that why he hadn't been back in several days, because he was working evenings on the marketing plan?

"You did?" I asked dumbly.

"Now that I know more about it, I want to help *save* your family's farm. Not kill it."

"But you'd lose your job."

He smirked. "I'll take that chance."

"Why?"

"Let's just say, it's time I start preserving my *own* legacy."

I couldn't keep the smile from my face. "Then you better have put together a damn good marketing plan."

# Chapter Twelve
## AUTUMN

"**G**randma, this is Braden," I said. "Braden, this is my Grandma Wanda."

Braden shook her hand and smiled at her. He was dressed in his familiar powder-blue shirt, tucked in to khaki pants this time—maybe that was his definition of "casual."

Maggie rushed up and sniffed him, but she must've sensed my nerves because she sat back and began to bark at him, which rocked her tiny body.

"Oh, Maggie, hush!" Grandma warned. She turned back to Braden with a smile. "It's nice to officially meet you. You've been coming to the orchard so often, it's almost like we've already met!"

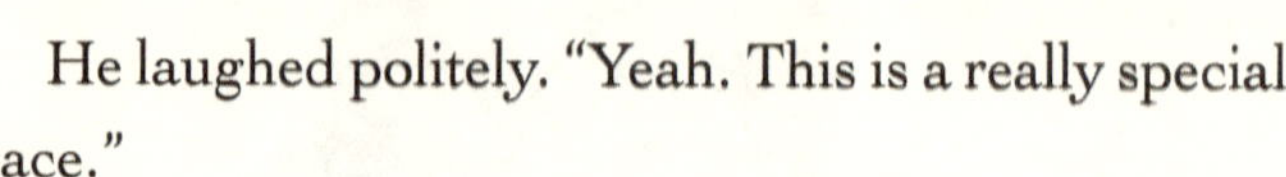



He laughed politely. "Yeah. This is a really special place."

"It certainly is." One of the pots on the stove began to bubble over and Grandma turned back to the kitchen quickly. "I need to finish up dinner. Why don't the two of you set the table?"

I nodded through the cased opening into the dining room. "You can take a seat, if you want. I'll grab the plates and everything."

Before he had a chance to make a choice, the door opened and both Uncle Stan and Uncle Jim walked in.

Again, Maggie rushed up to them, but after a few sniffs to confirm that they were who she thought they were, she backed off and returned to Grandma's side.

"This is almost ready, my dears," Grandma said. "Autumn, have you set the table yet?"

I rushed to the cabinet and began pulling down the plates. "Doing it now, Gram."

Braden shook both of my uncles' hands as I hurried around the table setting plates at each spot. Then, as I was rushing into the dining room with the silverware, he stopped me and took a handful from me so that he could help me finish placing them.

Uncle Stan and Uncle Jim helped Grandma bring over the food to the table and once we were all seated, we began to dig in.

"So, Braden, Autumn tells us you're interested in helping our farm?" Uncle Jim asked.

"Yeah—" Braden started, but Uncle Stan cut him off.

"Didn't you just present us with an offer to *buy it* from us a few weeks ago?"

"Um…yeah, I did," he said. "And, officially, I guess that offer still stands. But *personally*, there's an opportunity I'd like to talk to all of you about."

"Oh, after dinner," Grandma insisted. "We're not talking business on an empty stomach."

"Braden's been coming to the orchard almost every day," I told my uncles. "He's sort of been shadowing me and has seen a lot of the ways that we do things around here."

"You showed him *everything*?" Uncle Stan asked.

"Not everything," I assured him. "But a lot of the work we do and I've explained the thought processes that have gone into our decisions and business practices. He's even suggested a few that have really worked out well for us."

"Of course he has," Uncle Stan said. "He's trying to get you to—"

"That's enough, Stanley," Grandma warned. "I said no talk of business at the dinner table and I mean it. And we certainly are not going to make a guest feel uncomfortable in our home."

Uncle Stan let out a heavy sigh, then nodded.

Our silverware clinked as we quietly began to eat the breaded chicken and vegetables that Grandma had prepared.

Braden cleared his throat. "If I may, Miss…uh…*Grandma.*"

I couldn't help but chuckle at that, despite the awkward tension. I glanced over and saw Uncle Jim doing the same.

"Yes, dear?" Grandma asked.

"I would like to clear up some questions regarding my involvement here," Braden said. "I know it might feel…threatening to have me here, but I really do believe in your orchard. I love that this is a family business. And I'm sorry if you got the wrong impression of me personally when I presented that offer from my employer, but that's business. I was following a directive from my boss. Once I got here, I learned just how special Chapman Farms is. And I want to help you showcase that."

"*After* dinner," Grandma clarified. "First, we eat. Thank you, Braden, for such kind words about our little corner of the world."

I looked over at him and smiled.

We spent the rest of the meal awkwardly making small talk. Grandma asked Braden where he was from and what other accounts he worked with, but

the whole conversation was obviously one-sided.

By the time we were done eating, Uncle Stan eagerly told Braden to "get on with it" and so he pulled out a folder and began to talk.

Braden spoke passionately as he laid out the plans for his proposed Apple Festival. It was a strange feeling, having someone who was a complete stranger several weeks ago—a threat to Chapman Farms, even—now act almost as my savior. A fellow champion for our farm.

"It would be a total fall festival, centered around apples and, more specifically, your farm," Braden told my uncles as we sat around the dining room table. "Hayrides through the orchard, food trucks lined up in the parking lot, Chinese auction under a canopy—all donated by businesses right here in Medina, which would help build on the community morale that you've worked so hard to foster here."

Uncle Jim looked more excited than Uncle Stan, but they both sat quietly and let Braden talk.

"I've already taken the liberty of mocking up a flyer for it." He passed copies to me, my uncles, and Grandma Wanda.

The flyer featured apple trees prominently with *Chapman Farms Family Orchard* displayed across the top in fancy block lettering matching an old-timey feel that seemed to capture the simplicity of the farm

so well. Below, it announced dates and times of Apple Fest, as well as our address.

"Wow." Uncle Jim pulled on his glasses and studied it. "This looks really good."

"So creative!" Grandma Wanda said. "Did you design this?"

"I put some stuff together," Braden said shyly. "It's certainly not final, just a mockup, but I wanted to give you a better idea of the way that this would be marketed so that it aligns with your farm, as does the festival."

"This is all well and good, but how exactly are we going to spread word about this to a broader audience?" Uncle Stan asked.

Braden nodded and turned his paper over. "If you flip to the back, I've outlined the bulk of the marketing plan. Not only would we send press releases to traditional media—TV, radio, print—but we'd target a specific demographic with online ads, which would be the bulk of our budget."

Uncle Stan chuckled and shook his head.

Braden didn't falter, though. "I want to urge you to think of this as more of an investment into your business because, if we can pull this off, it'll continue to grow year-after-year and will become a mainstay in the Medina community for generations to come, especially once you start investing into improvements with your property by updating the house and the barn."

"You've worked very hard on this," Uncle Jim said. "And I appreciate that."

"I think a community festival is a fantastic idea!" Grandma added. "When I was a kid, it seemed like every weekend from Memorial Day through Christmas there was a chicken barbecue or lawn fete or meat raffle to go to. Nowadays, you don't see that anymore. Or, not as much. I would love to bring something like this back to the community."

Everyone seemed to turn to Uncle Stan for his appraisal of the proposal. As if he had more authority than any of the rest of us. Even Grandma Wanda, who wasn't *technically* a part owner, still had a lot of sway in the final decision-making of Chapman Farms.

Uncle Stan studied the plan while everyone talked. Finally, he set the paper down and crossed his arms as he leaned them down on the table. The gesture suggested that he had made his mind up about something. "I like the idea of investing in the property," he said. "Lord knows this old house could use some work. And I think that even if this Apple Festival thing doesn't take off like you hope it will, investing in the property would be a good investment because it would increase the value of the property

for when we go to sell it."

My heart sunk as he said the words with such assurance, as if it had already been decided.

"*If* we sell," Grandma interjected.

"Yeah, we don't know where this season's going to put us when all is said and done," I added.

Uncle Stan gave me a look, but moved on. "I'm just curious about the costs." He stared up at Braden. "You're a businessman. Talk money with me."

"I'm going to try to keep costs as minimal as possible, but that also depends on what kind of marketing budget we have." He slowly turned to me, and I knew that he felt guilty for putting me on the spot, but I was also the one who handled the day-to-day finances.

I stiffened in my chair, feeling the eyes from everyone in the room suddenly on me. "Well, um…it's not much." I chuckled nervously, trying to play it off as something humorous, even though nobody was laughing except me.

"I'm sure Mr. Clinton doesn't need any concrete numbers," Uncle Stan said, "just a ballpark."

I stared back at each of them, feeling their eyes like chains holding me to my chair.

"Do you need to run out to the office to check your book?" Grandma suggested.

"You could give me a figure later," Braden said, offering me a lifeline. "I can talk in general terms right now."

Uncle Stan held up his hand in Braden's direction, but kept his eyes on me. "No, I want to hear how much we have for marketing. She knows."

I tried to swallow, but my throat was dry. "Um…well, you see…I needed to move funds out of the marketing budget in order to pay for other things for the farm."

"So there's nothing in the marketing budget?" Uncle Jim asked.

I shook my head and lowered my eyes down.

"Could you move money from somewhere else?" Braden asked. "Maybe a reserve fund."

"We don't—"

"Huh?" Uncle Stan demanded. "You need to speak up. Tell us how you've completely liquidated our accounts and drained our cash flow."

"Stanley, that's enough!" Grandma said.

"Ma, she's—"

"—doing the best she can." Grandma stood and leaned on the table, daring him to challenge her further. "Whatever this distrust you have in Autumn, it doesn't have more to do with her gender—or her age—than it does with the farm, does it?"

"That's ridiculous, she's not *that* young and—" His mouth clamped shut as he realized he had unintentionally insulted me.

Not to be confused with when he did, in fact, insult me moments ago.

"No need to argue," Braden said. "For the purposes of the proposed Apple Festival, I can reach out to a couple investors I know and see if they can lend some money to this community-based project."

"That sounds like a good compromise," Uncle Jim said. "And may help us bring in some additional funds to replenish the accounts that Autumn has, um…*used*."

My heart felt heavy, but I kept my head held high. I had people in support of me, even if I was driving the business into the ground.

"You really know people who would be willing to give money for this?" I asked Braden.

He shrugged, shuffling around the papers he had brought. "Yeah, it's not a big deal. Businesses throw money at events all the time in exchange for some branding. We may need to add some logos to that flyer, but the focus will definitely be on Chapman Farms."

Uncle Stan cleared his throat. "Be that as it may, unfortunately we're facing the very *real* reality—" he glared over at me, "—that we will not be in

operation by this time next year. So, unfortunately, while I think this plan is nice, we're not going to be able to—"

"Oh, I understand the time constraints for this," Braden said. "That's why I was planning on hosting the Apple Festival *this* year."

The room fell quiet as his words sank in with everyone.

Uncle Stan and Uncle Jim exchanged looks…and then promptly burst out laughing.

I saw Braden shrink in on himself as some of his confidence deflated. I felt bad for him, especially since he was doing all of this to help us.

To help me.

I opened my mouth to defend him, but Grandma beat me to it.

"Would you boys cut it out!" she snapped. "I think we can pull it off. It sounds like Mr. Clinton has an excellent plan. Much better than the ones your father would've had. In fact, why don't we set a date right now so we can keep this momentum moving? How's Columbus Day weekend? That's one of our busiest weekends here at the orchard, and it's a three-day weekend, so more people are likely to want to go out and do something."

Braden nodded, offering my grandmother a smile. "That's exactly what I was thinking too."

I had my reservations about putting it all together and advertising enough to draw a sizable crowd in the short time we had left—just about five weeks—but I also wanted to prove my Uncle Stan wrong with all of his pessimism. Even if he was probably going to be right, in the end, about closing the farm.

"I think that's a good idea," I added, just so I could go against the grain with my uncle.

"Most people will be fully entrenched in the fall season by then, which Chapman Farms should be able to capitalize on if we do it right," Braden said. "If this is successful and you're able to keep the doors open, you might even consider hosting a spring or a summer festival down the line, especially once you get the barn renovated."

Uncle Stan waved him down, realizing that he was being outnumbered. "All right, all right. Let's worry about one thing at a time."

I celebrated the minor victory quietly.

"Do you really think you can get all of this done in just a few weeks?" Uncle Jim studied the marketing plan.

"It'll be a tight turnaround, and I'll need help, but I believe it can be done."

"Then you have my blessing. No sense in sitting back and not even *trying* to save the farm," he said.

I smiled, feeling a sense of hope that I hadn't felt in a while.

Uncle Stan, meanwhile, shook his head. "If you really think you can pull this off in such a short amount of time—and with investor money—then who am I to stop you?" He shrugged. "I just think that all of this is going to be a waste of time in the end."

"Nothing's a waste of time if you're really passionate about something." Braden looked over at me. "And I can tell your family is passionate about this farm—always have been. That's the charm and admiration that needs to shine during Apple Fest."

"All right." Uncle Stan slapped the table. "I need to be getting home. Good luck with this crazy dream of yours, kid."

"I'll walk you out. Cheryl's been texting me." Uncle Jim got up and gave Grandma a hug, then slapped me on the shoulder on his way to the door.

Uncle Stan followed suit, but when he said goodbye to me, he gave me a look. "If you get in over your head, don't be afraid to ask for help."

I nodded. Even though he was harsh, I knew he cared. I knew he loved me. And I knew he wanted to see the farm survive. But he was a realist at heart.

After my uncles left, Grandma rose to her feet as well and started to pick up from dinner.

"You convinced them," I told Braden as he collected the rest of his papers.

"Barely," he said. "Sorry about putting you on the spot. I didn't realize—I thought…I had no idea about the money thing."

I nodded. "It's my fault. Not exactly one of my proudest moments. Do you really think you can reach out to some investors?"

"Sure, no problem."

I wondered what it was like to operate in a world where, when you needed more money, you just asked for some and it showed up.

"And are you going to need to pitch this whole thing to them again?"

Braden finally met my eyes. "Just let me worry about it."

I let out a sigh. "I know. It's just not in my nature to trust anyone outside of the family with this business stuff. Especially when you're technically trying to take it all away from me."

"Technically," he said, but offered no other context. "We'll be fine. Have faith."

"That's hard to do. I mean, you saw firsthand what kind of pressure I'm under when it comes to the farm."

"Yeah, I see that now." He nodded to the door. "I should probably get going. I have a lot of work to do." He stepped around the corner into the kitchen and waved to Grandma. "Thank you for dinner, Wanda. It was delicious."

"If you save our farm, I'll make you dinner every day for the rest of my life."

"Easy there, Gram," I said.

She winked at me over her shoulder, then turned back to her dishes in the sink.

"I'll walk you out." I led Braden to the door, where we lingered. I felt like I owed him more than a thank you, but no other gesture seemed to fit.

"So," he started, "I guess I'll call you once I put together more of a concrete plan. I'll need a lot of your input on this, since you know the community so well."

"Anytime." I pulled out my phone. "What's your number?"

He stammered, but rattled off his number anyway.

I typed out a quick text and sent it to him. "There. Now we have each other's phone numbers. Text me whenever you have a question. I'm more likely to answer a text than a phone call. I have to keep up with the orchard and the customers."

He nodded. "Sounds like a plan."

We both still lingered, neither of us wanting to say goodbye, even though it was getting late and I

had an early wake-up call.

"I don't know how I'm going to make this up to you if you pull this off," I said. "Especially if it helps turn things around for Chapman Farms."

"Let's make sure it's a success before we start talking about repayment," he said. "But honestly, I'm glad I'm helping you. I can tell how much you and your family love this place, and I see the special beauty it has for your family—but also for the community. Unfortunately, I also see what happens to places like this by companies like mine. To tell you the truth, I hate it."

I thought about asking him why he still does it, but I knew why. The money was hard to turn down. And it helped him avoid the reality of the empty life left over by his late wife.

"Now that I see an opportunity to change, I know I need to take it." He took a small step closer to me and brushed my hair out of my face. "Plus, I like spending time with you."

I was suddenly consumed with him. The way he smelled, the heat of his body, the crease lines in his face when he smiled. "You do?"

Braden bit back his bottom lip between his teeth and it was suddenly the most attractive thing I'd ever seen. I felt myself leaning in, and saw him do the same—

Grandma's wails from deeper in the house broke up our tender moment.

Ripped from our bubble, we paused for the briefest moment before we both ran into the kitchen to see what was wrong.

"Grandma! What's going on?" I asked.

"She got out! She ran off! A critter's going to get her!" She was breathing heavy.

"Maggie?" I asked.

"Yes!"

"Okay," Braden said. "Just take a deep breath and sit down. We'll find her. Where do you think she ran off to?"

"I know," I told him. "I'll get her."

Braden dropped his bag by the wall. "I'll come with you."

Together, the two of us ran out the door.

# Chapter Thirteen
## BRADEN

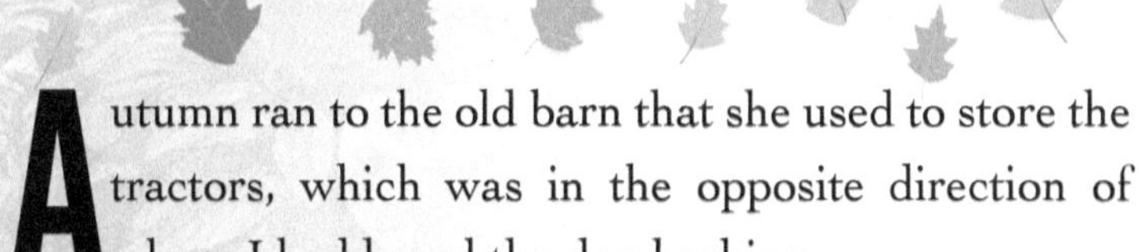

Autumn ran to the old barn that she used to store the tractors, which was in the opposite direction of where I had heard the dog barking.

"Where are you going?" I asked. "She went this way!"

"We won't catch her easily on foot." Autumn expertly climbed into the tractor seat. "Besides, she'll think it's a game if we start running after her." She fired up the engine, which made further communication at that distance impossible. Still, she waved me toward her and I ran to climb on.

I balanced my leather shoes on the worn metal rung and heaved myself upward with the help of Autumn's

outstretched hand. The only problem was, once I got up, I had nowhere to sit.

Autumn apparently didn't mind, and she hit the accelerator, sending me flopping back right into her lap.

She held her arm around me, which had prevented me from falling backward out of the seat. "Easy there. You all right?"

I nodded and sidled next to her as she drove, making sure more of my butt was on the seat than on her legs.

Autumn didn't seem to notice our close encounter, though. Her eyes were busy scanning the ground as she raced down the main path of the orchard, looking down the rows of trees.

I did the same on the other side, although between the speed we were going and the darkness, it was hard to distinguish what was what. Still, nothing seemed to be moving around among the trees. Not knowing what kind of wildlife lived in the orchard at night, I was both relieved and concerned.

Even with only a single headlight on the front of the tractor, Autumn navigated a turn down another wide path. Within minutes, we came up on a stream, where the rows of apple trees ended, giving way to a smaller path that was only a little wider than the width of the tractor.

She cut the engine and plunged us into darkness—and silence.

The wind blew, rustling leaves and grass as it moved across the earth. As time went on, my eyes adjusted to the darkness and I noticed—possibly for the first time—how many stars were in the sky.

"Wow," I muttered as my eyes drew upward.

Autumn followed my gaze, then looked back at me. "It's pretty amazing, isn't it? Not something you see in the city."

"Definitely not." I forced myself to focus back on what we had come back here for. "Are you sure this is where she was going? I don't hear anything." Another breeze came through, sending shivers up my spine. I hadn't rolled up the sleeves on my dress shirt, but it offered no insulation from the chilly fall evening temperatures.

"I'm sure." Autumn scanned the area. "This is where she's always running off to. She loves to play in the water." Suddenly, she stood and launched herself down to the ground with one leap.

I was sure I could do the same move if I tried, but it was still impressive to watch her move so gracefully in her element.

In her absence, though, I realized just how much her body heat had been warming me.

"Maggie!" Autumn called. "Maggie! Come here, girl!"

The sound of dog tags jangling suddenly became louder and, soon enough, we saw a tan-colored Yorkie running through the grass, illuminated by starlight. She ignored Autumn and ran straight for the stream.

Autumn dove and grabbed Maggie, just as her front paws hit the water. "Got you!" She pulled her close and rose to her feet. "Almost got away from me."

I watched as Autumn came around to the side of the tractor and handed the squirming Maggie up to me. I took her...and immediately felt a chill hit my center as the cold water from her front paws seeped into my thin shirt.

But the dog still wiggled, so even with goosebumps prickling my skin, I held her close as Autumn climbed up on the other side.

"Ever drive a tractor before?"

"No." I worked my free hand around the dog's head and gently stroked behind her ears, which seemed to calm her. "How different is it from driving a car?"

Autumn shrugged. "About the same. Just different."

"That's...not at all helpful."

She laughed.

"Well, I have her settled, so I think you should drive back," I told her.

"If you say so." She looked at me and our eyes locked. There, under the sky full of stars, with the stream trickling in the background, the moment was perfect.

But all good things came to an end, and that moment was no different. As my strokes behind her ears slowed, Maggie whipped around in my arms again, sending the water that had seeped into my shirt trickling down my skin, which drew involuntary shivers.

Autumn cleared her throat and turned back to the controls. "Let's get her back home where she belongs."

We zipped through the orchard, back to the house. The wind created by our speed only made me chillier, but I also didn't want the moment to end, sitting next to Autumn in the night. It was like, right there, out in the dark with no one else around, I had Autumn all to myself. And that, I was discovering, was something I wanted more of.

"**Y**ou found her!" Grandma Wanda called when we returned to the house. She scooped her out of my arms and began snuggling with her before pulling away. "Oh, Maggie, I was so—ugh! You're all wet!" She glanced over and saw me. The whole front of my shirt was soaked and wrinkled and clung to my skin. "And so are you!"

I looked down and tugged the cold, wet fabric away from myself. "It's okay. It'll dry."

Wanda put the dog down and waved her hand toward her. "Come on. Take off the shirt."

"Grandma!" Autumn said.

"He went out to help rescue my dog and got his clothes ruined in the process! The least I can do is wash it for him." She stepped forward and tried to reach for the top button.

I backed away, putting my hands out in front of me. Never before had I had an older woman try to take my clothes off. "No, it's okay. Really. I'm staying right in town. It won't be a far drive."

"And does this place have a washing machine?" Wanda pressed.

"Yeah, of course," I said. "I've been staying there for a month. That's why I've been wearing basically the same clothes every time you see me."

Beside me, I heard Autumn let out a soft, "Oh."

"Have you taken out stains like this before?" Wanda tugged at the side of my shirt. "Look at that muck all over yourself! You're going to get that shiny car of yours all dirty." She shook her head. "Take it off. I'll clean it for you."

"No, ma'am, it's really okay."

Wanda looked horrified.

"Oh, you've done it now," Autumn muttered.

I looked between them, confused.

"*Ma'am*?" Wanda put her hand on her hips.

"It's a…term of endearment?" I tried to plead my case. It wasn't working.

Wanda turned away, shaking her head. "Fine. Go stink up that car of yours. First you won't even let me thank you for saving my dog—not to mention the orchard—but then you call me *ma'am*? You are just trying to hurt me, aren't you?"

I knew it was an act. A bit theatrical and over the top, but I still felt bad for her. And I didn't want to hurt her. Not anymore than I already had.

Sighing, I began to unbutton my shirt. Luckily, I had a tank top T-shirt on under it, but it was still more vulnerable than I cared to be.

Once I placed the wet shirt in Wanda's hand, she smiled—until she saw my undershirt was wet too.

"No," I said firmer. "I'll let you wash that shirt, but not this one."

Beside me, Autumn giggled.

Wanda smirked and shrugged, then set off to the laundry room.

"Come on." Autumn nodded to the door. "Let's sneak out before she makes you take off your pants, too."

My face flushed and I was glad that Autumn had tuned her back to me so she didn't see it.

Outside, the chill hit my bare arms as we walked out to my car. Autumn pulled down the sleeves of her flannel and crossed her arms over her chest.

"You look cold," I told her.

"Not as cold as you." She released her stance and gently grazed her fingers over my goose bumped skin.

"I didn't think your grandma would strip me down in the kitchen."

"Sorry about that. I think she was trying to do that to help me."

"Help you? In what way?"

Autumn rolled her eyes. "My grandma likes to play matchmaker."

"She thinks there's a match here?"

"Apparently."

"And what do you think?"

She took in a deep breath. "I think…I think I like being around you. Even if you are my competitor.

And I'm grateful that you want to help me—help *us*—but…"

"But you're scared."

She nodded.

I ran my fingers down her cheek and tilted her chin up to face me. "I'm not going to hurt you." I leaned in, and when Autumn didn't pull away, I brought my lips to hers and kissed her softly. Finally finishing what I'd been meaning to do before Maggie ran away.

And suddenly I had goose bumps for a whole different reason.

I pulled away, even though it was clear we both wanted more, and opened my car door. "I'll see you tomorrow."

She smiled at that.

I got in the car and backed out of the driveway. Autumn stood where she was and watched me leave.

*Chapter Fourteen*
## BRADEN

The roar of the tractor met my ears when I stepped out of my car at Chapman Farms. Autumn was in the driver's seat, hauling the trailer with the wooden bench seats lining it. She came to a stop just behind the country store and I walked into the store to greet her as she came in.

The final customers of the day, who had just gotten off the hayride, filed out to their cars in the parking lot.

"Have a good night!" Autumn called after them as they left.

With the store empty, Autumn stepped behind the counter and punched a few buttons on the register, which popped open the drawer.

"How were sales today?" I asked.

She shrugged as she pulled out the bills and laid them out on the counter beside the register. "Not bad. It seemed to be steady." She held up the next wad of cash. "This will be the deciding factor." She pulled out a calculator from beneath the register and began to count out the day's earnings.

I wondered if maybe she felt awkward that we had kissed last night and that was why she didn't seem to stop moving. Then again, I was also getting to know Autumn and when she got into work mode she didn't seem to ever think about anything else. Part of the reason why I had stopped in. "Are you working tomorrow?"

She moved her lips as she counted quietly to herself. After she got to a point where she could type out the next number on the calculator, she looked up at me. "I work *every* day."

"Could you get out of it?" I asked. "Or maybe just for a few hours?"

She scrunched her eyebrows. "What are you getting at?"

I pulled the flyer from my back pocket and handed it to her.

She studied it, then looked up at me with skepticism. "A sock hop?"

"The swanky hotel across the street from where

I'm staying is hosting it," I said. "I thought it'd be fun."

"For *us*?" She handed the flyer back to me and shook her head. "No way." Back to the counting she went.

"Come on! It's dancing to fifties music in your socks! What's not to like?"

"I don't dance," she said quickly as she flipped through the bills.

"Neither do I," I said. "Not really, at least. But these things aren't about taking yourself seriously. It's about letting go and having fun."

She shook her head and kept her eyes on the money, typing another figure into the calculator.

"All right, look at it this way," I said, changing my approach. "You want to be more ingrained in the community for your business, right? What's a better way to do that than to show up to a *community* event without asking for anything in return? People see through a sales pitch, but if they view you as their friend and neighbor, then they'd be more likely to go out of their way to support you and your business."

Autumn finished counting and slammed the drawer closed. She tucked the stacks of bills, divided by denomination, in between her fingers as she carried them around back into the office.

I followed her around the corner and through the

door behind the counter.

"Can't I just support the community by being a regular shopper?" She sunk into her worn leather swivel chair and slid over in front of her computer. Setting the bills out carefully into stacks of their respective denominations, she turned to her computer and typed in her password.

"But that would be spending money over a long period of time." I sat on the corner of her desk. "Neither of those you have plenty of: time or money."

She shot me a look, then pulled out a deposit slip and began to write down the figures on it.

"Or you could spend twenty bucks, give up one evening, have *fun*, and make a huge impact on the community," I went on.

Autumn narrowed her eyes. "I don't do fun."

"I think it's time you start."

Another glare in my direction, followed quickly by a smile.

"I'll pay for your ticket," I offered. "All you'll have to be is my date."

She sighed. "What the hell do you even wear to a sock hop?"

Pulling into Autumn's house the next night felt like I was on a first date again. It had been almost ten years since I'd been on a first date and, even though I was now an adult, my heart hammered in my chest just as powerfully as it had been when I was fifteen and walking up to Sara's front door for the first time.

Up on the front porch, I rang the doorbell, even though I'd been invited to dinner on previous occasions.

Wanda opened the door and smiled when she saw me. "Why, hello, Braden. You look sharp!"

Autumn came around the corner looking nothing like she'd ever looked before, yet was still stunning. She wore a pink pleated poodle skirt and a white collared shirt. She had tall white socks and short black heels. Most transformative of all, though, was that her hair had been curled and pulled back into a tight ponytail that swung behind her as she moved.

My mouth hung open. "Wow. You look…you look great."

She crossed her arms and looked me up and down. "And you didn't put in any additional effort."

"Autumn!" Wanda scolded. "He looks very handsome, as always."

"Yes, *as always*. He could've at least opted for a different colored shirt."

I looked down at what I was wearing. My usual apparel: light-blue shirt, navy-blue tie, black slacks, and brown leather shoes.

Autumn turned and started back into the house, but I snatched her arm before she could get very far.

"Hold on!" I called.

"Honey, don't be rude," Wanda said. "This is sort of what men wore back in the day! Besides, people will be dressed all kinds of ways!"

"I hate this," Autumn murmured, conceding to my grip on her arm.

"I'll change," I told her. "I'm staying right across the street from where the sock hop is. It'll take me five minutes to put on something else."

Autumn sighed, then relented. "Okay."

Wanda hugged her granddaughter. "Have fun, my dear."

Autumn grumbled in response.

Outside, I could feel Autumn dragging behind as I led her by her hand to the car.

"Do you even know *what* you're going to wear?" she asked.

I stopped, pulled my tie over my head, and handed it to her. "Here, hold this." I began to unbutton my shirt.

Her eyes went wide. "Braden! You can wait until you're back at your hotel room!"

I ignored her and pulled off my blue shirt, revealing only my white T-shirt underneath. I had opted to wear this underneath my dress shirt more often now. Not only because of the chilling temperatures as we got later into the fall, but just in case I was ever forced to strip off my shirt at a moment's notice again. Tonight, however, that preparation came in handy. "Hold this."

She took it as she studied me.

I moved my hands around my waist, making sure my T-shirt was tucked into my slacks. When I was done, I held out my hands. "Huh? How's this?"

"How is that fifties?"

I held up my finger. "You're right." Bending over, I folded the bottom cuffs of my pants up twice so that my socks were showing. They were black—it would've looked more fifties if they were white—but they'd have to do. "Better?"

She sighed as she looked me over. "Well, at least I won't be the *only* one dressed like an idiot tonight."

The dance was busier than I thought it would be. And more diverse, in terms of ages. I half-expected Autumn and I to be some of the youngest people there. I thought we'd be spending the evening making fools of ourselves in front of people who were trying to relive their youth.

While those people were in attendance, the larger part of the crowd was made up of people our age. Some were dressed in similar outfits to us, others were in pastel-colored suits, and all of them were in their socks.

Autumn greeted so many people with smiles and hugs. She approached one woman, who was wearing a wide red dress with white polka dots. It had black lace peeking out underneath, and she wore a black shirt with a white collar underneath. To top it off, the woman had very dramatic makeup around her eyes with bright red lips.

"Braden, this is Louise!" Autumn told me. "She and her husband own the pharmacy downtown."

"Autumn! I didn't think you'd be here!" Louise's face was wide with surprise.

Autumn waved off the idea. "Oh, Braden convinced me."

"Is he…are you two…?" Louise's unfinished question hung in the air.

"He's been a regular at the orchard," Autumn said, stepping carefully around any lies. "He thought this would be fun, so he invited me along."

"Autumn Chapman!" a booming voice called across the room.

We turned to see a burly man stepping toward us. He wore a red letterman jacket that was far too small for him and a white T-shirt underneath that clung tightly to his prominent belly. The attempt to emulate his teenaged years only made the elderly man look a little sad. But the outfit was fitting for the event.

"Victor!" Autumn had a big smile on her face as she hugged him. "Oh, my gosh, I haven't seen you in forever! How are you?"

He nodded. "Good. Good. How's everything at the farm? Still keeping up your grandpa's legacy?"

"Something like that," she said.

"How's your grandma?"

"She's good. Just as kooky as always."

He laughed. "She always knows how to keep everyone on their toes!"

Autumn responded with a laugh.

Victor turned to me. "And you are…?"

"I'm a friend," I blurted, offering my hand.

He shook it as Autumn explained who he was.

"Victor was good friends with my grandpa. He actually used to work at the farm when I was younger."

"My family and the Chapmans go way back," he explained.

The music started, drowning out any chance of

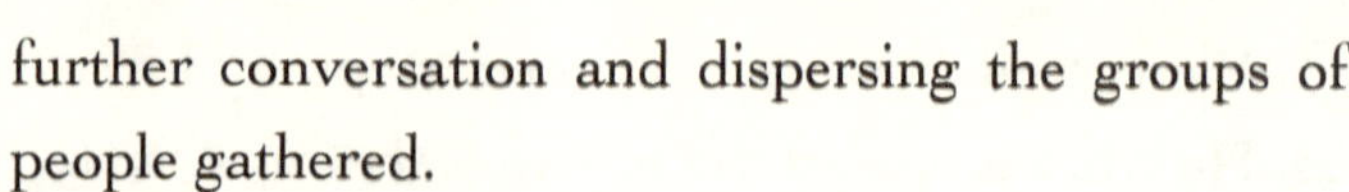



further conversation and dispersing the groups of people gathered.

Autumn and I kicked off our shoes by the wall and moved to the dance floor with everyone else in their socks and began to dance to the tunes of the forties, fifties, and sixties.

My date's body was stiff as she danced. Her eyes scanned the room, as if trying to decipher what everyone was thinking of her.

I hooked my hand around her waist and leaned in close to her ear so she could hear me. "Nobody's paying attention to you. Besides, you're more likely to draw eyes by *not* dancing. Relax." I held her hands and helped her move more naturally to the music. By the time the next song started, she was smiling and moving her body easily to my lead.

Some of the dancers were really into the sock hop. Others clearly had been practicing the retro dances in anticipation of this event. The jitterbug, the boogie-woogie, and the twist were all very prominent. Autumn and I, however, just kept to whatever felt right with the beat of the music.

With so many people in the room—especially on the dance floor—we needed a break after a while. I led Autumn over to the bar, which was crowded with people. Worse, our socks began to stick to the floor the closer we got to the bar.

Alcohol made grown adults extra sloppy.

I leaned down to Autumn's ear. "Want to go downstairs and get a drink? We can have a little more privacy there."

She nodded and I took her hand and led her back to find our shoes.

Downstairs, we crossed the street and stepped into the little shop that was tucked into the storefront right next to the hotel I'd been staying at. It was both a café and a cocktail bar and it had a vintage feel, but in a more elegant style than the blatant fifties-inspired dance across the street.

We ordered our drinks—an espresso martini for Autumn and a spiked coffee for me—then carried them toward the back of the shop where we could have some relative privacy in a booth.

"So on a scale of one to ten, how miserable was it for you tonight?" I asked her.

"Well, at the risk of you thinking that I want to do it again, I did actually have fun."

My eyes widened and I clamped a hand over my heart as I dramatically dropped back in my seat. "*You're* capable of *fun*?"

"Ha. Ha," she deadpanned. "Read my lips: never again."

I sipped my coffee and felt both the warmth from the hot liquid and the burn from the bourbon fill my body. "Never say never."

To my surprise, she laughed at that. "I think it's only fair that I pay you back," she said.

"In what way? A waltz?"

Another laugh. Man, she was feeling relaxed tonight. It was a nice look on her.

"Do you think I'd trade one dance for another when you know I hate dances?" she asked. "Sounds like torture to me. No, I want to put you through something equally as uncomfortable as tonight was for me."

"So then what did you have in mind?"

She shook her head. "Nope. You didn't give me much warning for this, so I won't give you much warning for whatever it is that I come up with."

"Just as long as it's not humiliating." The last thing I needed was for something to get spread on social media. If Mr. Ramsey found out that I was up in Medina schmoozing with the owner of Chapman Farms—especially if he found out that I was *helping* her with the business—then I would most definitely be fired. Never mind that stupid Director of Acquisitions title.

She shrugged. "Tonight had the potential to be very humiliating for me, so you never know."

"Play nice."

"Do you really think I wouldn't?" There was a

playful smile on her face that was very seductive. I couldn't decide whether she was doing it on purpose or not.

"So you're not going to give me any indication as to what this uncomfortable experience might be?" I asked.

"Nope."

"Well." I did my best to return her smile with the same energy. "I look forward to seeing what you come up with."

# Chapter Fifteen
## BRADEN

**H**enry was having the time of his life. He was currently running around the leaf-covered yard, leading a pack of other kindergarteners as they chased him to get the ball back.

The luxuries of being six years old at your birthday party. If only I could go back to a time to when I was so unbelievably happy with life.

I sat on the deck even after my in-laws had moved their seats. Or maybe they were my *former* in-laws? It was hard to determine exactly what Sara's family was to me now that she was gone.

Both of Sara's parents had moved their patio chairs to the lawn to watch the kids run around better. All of

them—kids and adults included—laughed with excitement. The rest of the parents gathered around down by the grill, beside the coolers, even though with the chillier fall temperatures, it wasn't like the coolers were absolutely necessary. They chatted with Bernie, who was watching to make sure the party was running smoothly.

Lenny came out onto the deck through the sliding door carrying a plate of meat, which he passed off to Bernie, who was manning—or *wo*manning—the grill.

"You need another drink, Brady?" he asked once his hands were free.

I lifted my drink and shook it a little to measure its contents. "Uh, sure. Just a water. Thanks."

"You got it." He raced down the stairs to the cooler.

My phone buzzed with another text and, with the momentary reprieve from social obligations, I looked at it. It was from Autumn.

We'd been texting back and forth all week about the upcoming Apple Festival. With the decisions that needed to be made, it was nice to have her immediately available to answer quick questions. Since the event was going to take place at Chapman Farms, a lot of people had been calling there with inquiries instead of my number, like had been listed on the application.

JUST GOT ANOTHER CALL FROM A VENDOR ASKING ABOUT PRICES AND DATES.

SORRY ABOUT THAT. I WISH THEY WOULD JUST CALL ME LIKE IT SAYS.

IT'S OKAY! I'M GETTING EXCITED.

I smiled. There was newfound enthusiasm to all of my interactions with Autumn lately. We hadn't talked about that kiss we shared a while ago, so I doubted her happiness was because of that, but whenever I stopped over she seemed more hopeful for the future. Less grim about the outlook of the orchard, even while there was a sense of guardedness as to whether this was the magic pill that would solve everything.

I doubted it would be the solution to *everything*. But it was a start.

"Who are you texting that you're smiling down at your phone so much?" Lenny's voice startled me as he came back up onto the deck and handed me the promised drink.

I turned my phone face-down on the table and straightened up in my seat. "Nobody. Just work stuff."

Lenny hooked an eyebrow behind his sunglasses.

Late September was a weird blend of summertime activities mixed with fall weather. We were out enjoying a barbecue while donning hooded sweatshirts and jackets.

"Since when does work stuff make you smile like that?" He popped the top of his beer off and took a sip.

I shrugged and opened my own drink, which was dripping with melted ice from the cooler. It made my hands cold and I wiped the excess moisture onto my jeans before burrowing my hands into my pockets. "I guess I'm just excited about this project."

"Is this still the Chapman Farms account?"

I nodded.

"And is the part that's making this exciting the *bitch* of an owner?"

I nearly choked on my water. I forgot I had called Autumn that. I used my sleeve to wipe up the extra water from my chin. "Uh, yeah. She's not so bad after all."

Lenny didn't look convinced, but he sat back in his seat and took another sip of his beer. "Uh-huh. So you're *not* seeing her?"

"No. Not...officially." It was hard to pinpoint exactly *what* was going on between me and Autumn, but I knew we were definitely *not* together and I

knew that I didn't want to have this conversation with my late wife's brother.

"But you want to be *official*?"

I shrugged again. "I don't know. The only other girl that I ever dated was your sister, and that was so long ago that it's hard to remember. Things are different now."

"Every relationship is different, no matter what happened between you and Sara."

"Nothing *happened*, Len," I blurted. "She died."

That poignancy soured the conversation for a minute. From the yard, Bernie called to Henry to let the other kids have a turn with the ball. My nephew's selective hearing was acting up and he was not interested in heeding to his mother's rules.

"So tell me about this girl," Lenny said.

"She's nice."

"Lots of girls are *nice*. What makes this one different?"

I shrugged. Again. Was I getting a workout in with this conversation? "I don't know. She's different."

Lenny blew out a breath. "Woo. Nice *and* different. I can see why you like her."

I couldn't help but laugh. "Shut up."

The truth was, whatever was going on between me and Autumn, I wanted to protect it. Even if it was

just a one-time kiss, I didn't want to jinx the potential for something bigger that might be there.

"Well, whatever you see in her, I'm glad you're finally moving on," Lenny said.

"You are?" I looked over at him. "You realize, I'm moving on from *your sister*."

"I know. I've kind of been following along, remember?"

Sara's loss had been felt just as hard by Lenny as it had been by me. But it had been a year and a half since she passed. A lot of the "firsts" without her had already happened. It was time to start letting life go on.

"You deserve to be happy," Lenny said. "And if this girl makes you happy, then I'm happy for you. Maybe someday we'll get to meet her."

The idea of introducing Autumn to Sara's family put knots in my stomach.

But that was crazy. Autumn and I kissed *one* time. There'd been no promise of anything more than that, especially in the last several times we'd seen each other. Sure, our banter had changed from one of contention to one of collaboration, but that was only because we had a common goal we were working toward.

Not to mention, it was crazy of me to think about a future with anyone else while I sat among Sara's

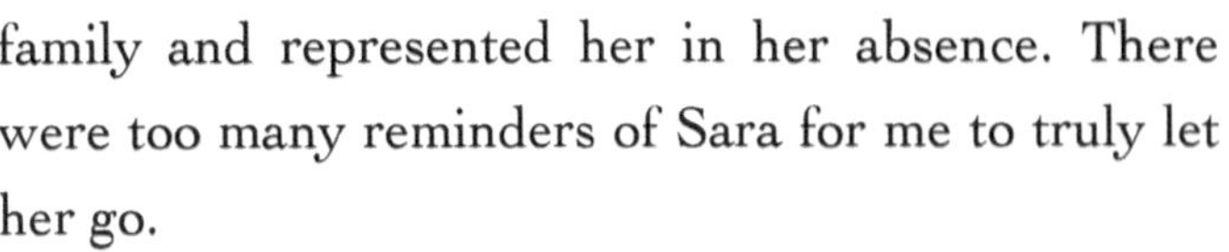

family and represented her in her absence. There were too many reminders of Sara for me to truly let her go.

# Chapter Sixteen
## AUTUMN

"**Y**ou were right about one thing," Braden said as we walked over to take our spots at the stalls, each of us carrying archery bows, "this place is *definitely* out of my comfort zone."

I eyed up the attendant who accompanied us back to the shooting ranges at the back of the property. He stood a good distance away, talking with someone else who came to practice shooting.

"You don't like it here?" I tried to keep the enthusiasm out of my voice, but there was no denying the smirk on my face.

"You mean the backroad location or the fact that this place looks like something out of a horror movie?"

I looked around. There were six-foot wooden stalls built in a line at the edge of the shooting range and a grassy berm built up around the perimeter of the range. Sure, there was a ramshackle-looking shed near the range, but I had to guess that was only where the owners kept things like the lawnmower and other things like that. Or maybe it was the dirt road that led to the back of the property for the shooting range that was putting Braden off.

Either way, I had successfully gotten him back for that sock hop.

"Come on," I said. "These are nice people."

"Maybe so, but I stick out like a sore thumb."

True to form, Braden wore his powder-blue shirt and black pants. He did look good, but it was not necessarily archery attire, and it showed with the way the owners and the other customers looked at him when we walked up.

"It's okay," I said, gloating. "It's clear you're a beginner. Don't feel bad. The guys here will help you, no matter how you're dressed."

We stepped up to our stalls, where there was a set of arrows stored in a PVC pipe that acted as a sort of quiver. It had been screwed to the edge of the stall wall with a bracket.

"I have to warn you, though," I went on, "my uncles and my dad used to take me out hunting and fishing all the time. They very clearly wanted a boy in the family, but I held my own. Still do, so don't feel bad if I'm doing a better job than you. You'll get it eventually, if you stick with it."

"Then why don't you go first and show me how it's done?" he suggested.

I grabbed an arrow from the makeshift quiver, nocked it in place, then pulled back on the string as I lined up my sight. Keeping my arms still, I released the string from my one hand and the arrow soared through the air, driving it right into one of the red rings on the target near the berm. Looked to be about the seventh ring, from what I could tell at that distance.

"Very nice," Braden said from behind me.

Showing off, I grabbed another arrow and fired it right at the same ring, but a little higher. That was my usual hit, although I had hit the bullseye several times when I was a teenager and my dad took me out target practicing regularly. I was very much out of practice, though.

"You want to try?" I asked him.

"I can *try*," he said. "I'm not really sure what I'm doing."

"Do you want some help?"

"I think I can figure it out."

I stood just outside of his stall while he lined up

the arrow. He raised the bow up, pulled back on the string, and released it.

His arrow ripped through the air and landed right in the gold ring. The outer tenth. The next one in was the bullseye.

My mouth hung open. "You totally played me!"

He turned and shrugged, even though a smile was plastered on his face. "I was in the archery club in high school."

I scoffed and marched over to my stall to reload. As I was setting up my next shot, another arrow flew out of Braden's stall and, to my horror, landed right in the center of his target.

"Jerk," I murmured.

"What was that?" He tapped on the wall separating our stalls. "I couldn't hear you!"

Ignoring him, I fired my next shot, which of course completely missed the target altogether.

I was letting my nerves get the better of me.

My next shot wasn't any better, landing in the grass just before the target.

"You want to hit that big circle out there," Braden teased.

"I know, I know!" I grabbed another arrow, shoved it into place, raised the bow, pulled back on the string and —

*Snap!*

"Ahh!" I called out and dropped my bow to the ground as I clutched my stinging arm.

Braden was beside me in an instant, as was the attendant who had followed us back to the shooting range.

"Are you okay, miss?" he asked.

Braden pulled my hands toward him and inspected both of them. His eyes finally settled on my wound. There was a large red mark along the inner part of my forearm from where the string had grazed it. It was a stupid injury. One a rookie made with improper form, and yet here I was.

"I'm fine," I said.

"We should get this checked out," Braden said.

"I'm *fine*." I was embarrassed for the injury, but also annoyed. Not only that Braden seemed to be good at everything, but also that I was pouting about it like a little kid.

The fact that Braden's powder-blue shirt had a big rip in it helped alleviate my annoyance.

"What happened to you?"

He glanced down at his shirt, having just noticed it himself. "You screamed just when I released my arrow. I guess the string caught my shirt."

I smiled. At least there was one chink in his armor.

"Come on," the attendant urged. "We need to

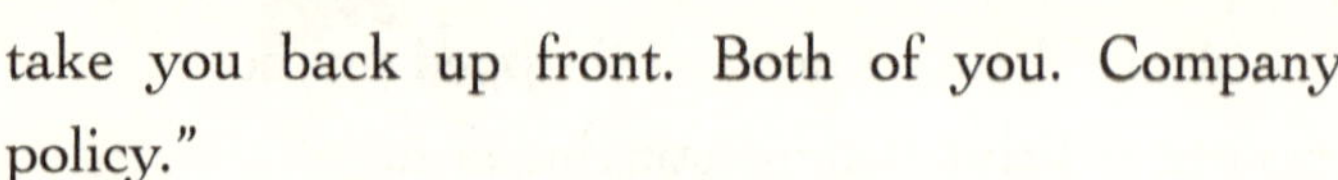

take you back up front. Both of you. Company policy."

Knowing that I wasn't going to enjoy any more of this archery outing, I followed the attendant.

**C**all it even?" Braden asked.

We were back in town, eating at a pizzeria-slash-bar on Main Street. Our alcoholic beverages sat in front of us—apple bourbon for me, seasonal lager for Braden. We had ordered a pizza, but it hadn't come yet.

"Call what even?" I asked.

"Our very short-lived rivalry," he said. "Of trying to see who could make the other more uncomfortable."

I nodded. "Oh. That. Yeah, I guess we can call it even. Although, somehow, I was the one who was made most uncomfortable both times."

"I don't know about that," he said. "At least you were dressed appropriately both times."

"Should I bust out the poodle skirt the next time we go to the shooting range?"

He raised his eyebrows. "Oh, so there'll be a next time? Figured you wouldn't want to be humiliated a second time."

"I have to redeem myself sometime," I fired back. My eyes flicked down to his shirt, which still flapped back and forth from the tear. "Sorry about that."

Braden looked down at it and shrugged. "It's all right. I have others."

I rolled my eyes. "Yeah, you probably have a whole closet full of those blue shirts."

He laughed and took a sip of his drink.

"What's with that anyway? You wearing the same shirt all the time."

"A lot of brilliant people wear the same shirt every day," he said. "It's one less thing to have to decide and helps you focus on other, more important things."

I eyed him, not buying his reasoning.

"Okay," he said. "I just like blue. Actually, that style shirt was one Sara used to tell me she liked on me. But I promise I have other clothes at home. I just didn't bring them all to my hotel here in Medina."

My finger traced the rim of my glass as we fell into a comfortable silence.

"Can I...ask you a question about your wife?" I braved.

"Sure. What do you want to know?"

I shrugged. "I don't know. Other than the fact

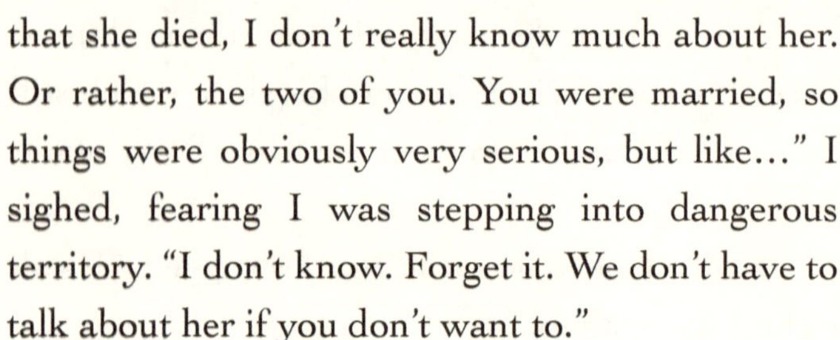



that she died, I don't really know much about her. Or rather, the two of you. You were married, so things were obviously very serious, but like…" I sighed, fearing I was stepping into dangerous territory. "I don't know. Forget it. We don't have to talk about her if you don't want to."

"No, I don't mind," he said. "Actually, it's nice to talk about her."

"Okay…" I took a breath before I started. "Did you guys plan to have a family? Were you trying to? I know you said you used to work at a non-profit, so you probably didn't have a lot of money, but that doesn't mean…" I trailed off. I was rambling now.

"Yeah, we wanted a family," he said. "In fact, we were trying when Sara's health started to take a turn for the worst. We thought we would get a handle on that before we tried again, but that obviously never happened."

I stared into his eyes. "I'm sorry."

He shrugged. "Thanks, but it's not your fault. Things with me and Sara just…weren't meant to be forever. And that's okay. I've dealt with that." Then, he corrected. "Actually, I'll *always* be dealing with that, but I have to move on."

I smiled. "Sounds like you two were very happy together."

"We were," he said. "And I miss her. But my life continues, even if hers doesn't."

The waitress came over with our pizza, which put a firm end to our heart-to-heart conversation.

# Chapter Seventeen
## AUTUMN

"So, tell me, what inspired this event?" asked Sharon Maybrook. She was a reporter from the online newspaper that covered everything in the county.

"Well, um…" I looked down and eyed the microphone that was poised on the picnic table between us. We were sitting out in the orchard. It was Tuesday, so there was virtually nobody at the farm. "The orchard is hitting a bit of a rough patch and we were trying to brainstorm ideas of what else we could do, not just for us, but for the community, and the idea for an annual Apple Festival came up, which seemed like a good idea."

I did my best to remember everything that Braden had coached me on:

*Keep the focus on the farm.*

*Make mention that you're struggling, but do not discuss money.*

*Emphasize that this event is for the* community *and not just a handout.*

I'd never sent press releases before, but Braden had insisted that it was one of the best ways to get the word out about the upcoming Apple Festival. Luckily, he had drafted one up and had me send it from my email so that it was as if I had written it myself. While I had gotten a lot of responses from contacts asking for further clarification about different things, Sharon was the only one who had reached out to do a full story.

"You're certainly putting this together with a very quick turnaround," Sharon said. "Have you gotten a lot of interest so far?"

"We've had a lot of interest, yeah," I said honestly. "We already have some great vendors lined up, as well as a lot of fun family-friendly activities."

A couple more Braden-isms:

*Don't mention the specific number of vendors unless it's more than fifty.*

*Make sure to mention that this event is intended for the whole family.*

At the moment, I wished that Braden was with me. Or, better yet, that he was doing the interview instead of me.

The truth was, we'd gotten a lot of interest from vendors, but very few sign-ups. More often, we had gotten, "I wish I could, but I'm already booked that weekend" or "If it wasn't the three-day weekend I would" or "Let me know how it goes and maybe we can do it next year."

The whole thing had been pretty discouraging, but the community interest in attending was nice. Still, I wished that that *interest* would translate into *action*.

"It sounds like it'll be a fun time," Sharon said. "Is this your first time planning such a big event?"

"It is, yeah," I said. "But I have some great help. My grandma has been a huge support. She's planning on baking all kinds of delicious things that we'll have on sale here in the store. Not mention, of course, the apples, which should be in full bloom by that weekend. We'll have some yard games and awesome vendors and hayrides. It'll be fun. I'm looking forward to it."

"I am, too! I will definitely be here to report on it." She stood, and I followed suit.

I offered a polite smile but, in truth, I was panicking. What if the event wasn't a success? What

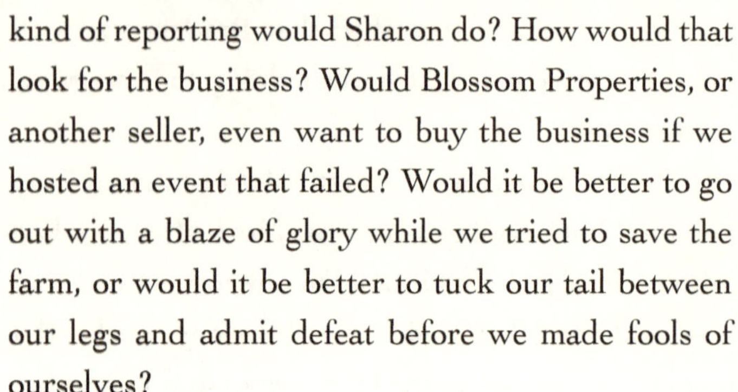



kind of reporting would Sharon do? How would that look for the business? Would Blossom Properties, or another seller, even want to buy the business if we hosted an event that failed? Would it be better to go out with a blaze of glory while we tried to save the farm, or would it be better to tuck our tail between our legs and admit defeat before we made fools of ourselves?

I walked Sharon back to her car and we shook hands.

"Thank you for coming out," I told her. "I appreciate all the press we can get about this. I hope we'll get a big turnout."

"It's ambitious, I'll give you that," Sharon admitted. "But you guys have been such a staple in Medina, and in Orleans County in general, that I think you'll see a lot more support than you realize."

I laughed nervously. "Let's hope so!"

After Sharon got in her car, I went back into the store, where Braden was chatting with Grandma, who was standing behind the counter.

"So? How'd it go?" he asked right away.

"I think it went well."

"Did you mention all the things Braden told you to mention?" Grandma asked.

"Yes. And I tried to make it seem very natural, too." I looked over at Braden. "Please tell me we've gotten more confirmations from vendors.”

Braden shook his head. “No more so far. I’m sorry.”

I sighed.

“Don’t stress, dear,” Grandma told me. “We’ll get more. Have faith.”

“Will we get enough?” I motioned out to the parking lot, where Sharon had just driven away. “We’re promising a fun day for everyone, but will we be able to deliver on it?”

“Have faith,” Grandma persisted. “We’ll just have to make sure we make as many good treats so everyone leaves happy and comes back a little fatter.”

Braden snickered.

“Especially you!” she added. “Speaking of, I need to go inside and start looking through old recipe books, see if I can find something that’ll work for our Apple Festival.” She came around the counter and, as she passed by me, put her hands on either side of my cheeks, leaned my head down, and planted a kiss on my forehead. “You’re a smart, hardworking young woman. You’ll figure this out. I believe in you. Let me know what else I can help with.” She turned to our guest. “Braden, as always, it’s been a pleasure.”

After she left, my shoulders slumped. “I hope she’s right.”

Braden stepped toward me and put one of his

hands on my shoulder. It was a strange form of contact, given our brief history, although his touch and close proximity did send a rush through me. "We're doing the best we can."

"What if our best isn't good enough?"

I found myself stepping closer to him, leaning against his chest for comfort. We hadn't discussed anything about that kiss last week, but this felt…right. Even if I did feel like I needed to hide it from my grandma. She would either get the wrong impression —that we were forbidden lovers, which of course we were *not* —or she would warn me to tread carefully, knowing that Braden was still the competition. She might even feel guilty for pushing me to use romance to learn a thing or two about saving the business once she learned that *real* feelings were starting to bubble between us.

Maybe.

Possibly.

"Have you noticed any uptick in customers this season?" Braden wrapped his arms around me.

It was intimate, but it worked. It felt easy. Even while it confused the heck out of me.

"Um…not really. Well…" I thought about it some more. We had repainted the sign on the old barn, the one that had advertised Chapman Farms as people pulled into the parking lot. It gave the whole orchard a refreshed feel it hadn't had before.

We had also put out a bonfire ring outside the shop that encouraged people to sit and relax, and we offered warm apple cider as the weather turned colder. Grandma even began giving out samples of the baked goods, which had increased sales.

And that wasn't to mention the small changes that Braden had suggested that had improved traffic flow—the fence by the parking lot, the door leading right from the store out to the orchard, and hayrides to the deeper parts of the orchard.

Added up, it was making a small improvement to our regular sales. But it wasn't enough.

"Things are getting better," I told him. "But not soon enough."

"Hopefully the vendor show will help turn it around."

"You've secured the investors?"

He nodded. "All set with that."

"Now we just need to worry about the vendors."

"I don't want you to worry about that at all. I'll take care of it. I'll cast a wider net, call in some favors. I've got this. I've got you."

His words struck deeper than I expected. Even though we had grown closer—physically, as we held each other, but also building on our relationship, whatever it may be—I suddenly realized that I was

completely trusting my rival.

But what other choice did I have?

"You would do that for me?" I asked.

"Of course I would."

# Chapter Eighteen
## BRADEN

I was burning the candle at both ends and it was showing in my job performance. No longer was I the all-star employee of Blossom Properties that I had been. Now, I was delivering reports right on time instead of early, or sometimes I would even turn them in late. I was often distracted by my phone, which was constantly buzzing with texts and emails as people replied to my inquiries to participate in the Apple Festival at Chapman Farms. Not to mention that I often felt my eyelids grow heavy while sitting at my desk, which was something I hadn't felt since Sara had been sick.

I continued clicking around on my computer, adding in numbers to the correct cell on the spreadsheet so I could send it over to the next department to shuffle information around before it was presented at a meeting and promptly forgotten in favor of the next report that needed to be done *immediately.*

"Clinton!" Mr. Ramsey's harsh voice boomed over the wall of my cubicle and startled me. I didn't notice him approach.

"Yes, sir?"

"In my office." He nodded his head in the direction of his office, then marched off toward it, not offering any other explanation.

Like a kid going off to see the principal for a punishment, I obliged and followed along to Mr. Ramsey's office, feeling everyone's eyes on me as I passed by the other cubicles.

Due to the scrutiny, I took the liberty of closing the door behind me.

"Have a seat." He indicated the chair across from his desk while he shuffled papers around that had been cluttered around his computer.

"Is everything okay, sir?" I asked once I was seated.

"What's been going on with you?"

"What do you mean?"

"What do you mean, what do I mean?" he asked. "You've been showing up later and later, leaving just a little early each day, and when you *do* show up you look exhausted. Reports are getting done, but they're not on time. Clinton, you've got several people concerned. Are you on drugs?"

My eyes widened. "Drugs? No!" I was glad I had closed the door. "I've just been burned out a little, trying to keep up with my job here and going up to Medina to try to secure the Chapman Farms account."

"Oh yeah." Mr. Ramsey tossed the papers he'd been holding onto his desk, then leaned back in his chair. "How's that going? Securing that account? Is the owner—what's her name? Autumn Chapman?—is she still giving you a hard time?"

"They're, um…still adamant about keeping the farm, yes." I wanted to stay as close to the truth as I could. "Things are progressing."

"I would think, as we're getting closer to the end of apple season, that she'll really start to see the writing on the wall."

I nodded. "Yes, that's definitely on her mind."

Mr. Ramsey raised his eyebrows, apparently finding deceit in something I had said. "I see that they're advertising an Apple Festival in a few weeks."

"Yes, that's their latest attempt to keep the farm." I hated talking down about the farm and the Chapmans in general, but in order to keep my job I needed to play along.

Mr. Ramsey took a deep breath and let it out slowly while he studied me. "It's funny. That's exactly the same thing we did after we acquired a family apple orchard out in Ohio. It helped build community morale, allowed people to believe that the orchard was still a place that they could find nostalgia, and helped us quell any objections to our buying it. That strategy worked well for us."

"Yes, sir, it did." I interlaced my fingers, forcing them to remain still so I didn't show any signs of nerves.

"You're not helping them put that together, are you?"

Here was my first lie to Mr. Ramsey. "No, sir, I'm not."

"Good. I want you to do everything in your power to make sure that show is a complete and total failure."

I nodded, even though all of my muscles felt stiff from the stress. I was glad I kept my phone on my desk—face down. With the way it had been buzzing all morning, I almost definitely had gotten a notification during this meeting.

"I'll get the account, sir," I told him.

"Good. Your new title is riding on it."

My nerves hadn't settled all day, and when I pulled into the parking lot for the hotel in Medina, I was glad to finally be in the familiar, comforting place that this little town had become.

At the front desk, I rang the bell and summoned Micah from the back.

"Mr. Clinton! How are you today?" he asked with a wide smile.

"Doing pretty good," I said. "I'd like to renew my stay for another month, if I could." With the Apple Festival planned for the middle of October, I knew I'd be overpaying by two weeks, but I also needed to watch my finances better as my cash had recently been depleted by quite a bit.

"We can certainly do that for you." He logged in to his computer, which sat on the small counter that served as the reception desk. "Are you planning on moving in?"

I laughed. "Tempting, but no. I'm here on business."

"Business? I can't imagine what business would require you to stay in Medina for two months, but I suppose *that* business is none of *my* business." He told me the total for the next month.

Another polite laugh as I handed him my credit card. "I'm from Blossom Properties and I was sent

here to try to get Chapman Farms to sell their business—and their property to us but—"

I was cut off when my phone rang. It was the call I had been waiting for all day.

"Percy, hi!"

Percy Langston was a manager for the Running Dolls, a local band out in Buffalo. They had been gaining a decent-sized following and I had put in a call to see if the band could play at the Apple Festival.

Micah finished running my card and handed it to me, then presented a receipt and a pen to me.

"Braden, I got your call." Percy's voice already sounded sympathetic and I braced myself for the let down.

I propped the phone against my ear as I signed the receipt for Micah, then offered him a quiet, "Thanks," and a wave as I headed for the stairs up to my room.

"And?" I asked into the phone.

"And I'm not sure we'll be able to make it work," he said. "You know I'd love to help you out. Over the years, you've put together a few events that have really been great at building the band's following, but I don't know about this one. We're already booked for the night before and the boys need some time off because we'll be traveling the following week."

I dug my key out of my pocket and unlocked the door. "Come on, Percy, there's nothing you can do for me? I really need you guys there."

"I'm sorry, bud."

"What if I offered to increase the payment?" I sat at the small dining table, opened my laptop, and pulled up my bank account information. It had been drained pretty considerably with all the spending I'd been doing on advertising for the Apple Festival.

"How much?"

I sighed as I looked over my funds. "What if I gave you an extra thirty percent?"

"Thirty percent! You sure you can swing that?"

"I think it's in my budget." Being the angel investor had its downsides, but seeing how happy Autumn would be if and when this festival turned out to be a success would be worth it. And the band was going to be a big part of that success.

"Let me talk to the boys and I'll get back to you."

"Thank you, Percy! I really appreciate it."

I got off the phone and sat back in the chair. I looked out the large windows and at the blue sky above. I was definitely sticking my neck out for Chapman Farms. I just hoped Sara was looking out for me.

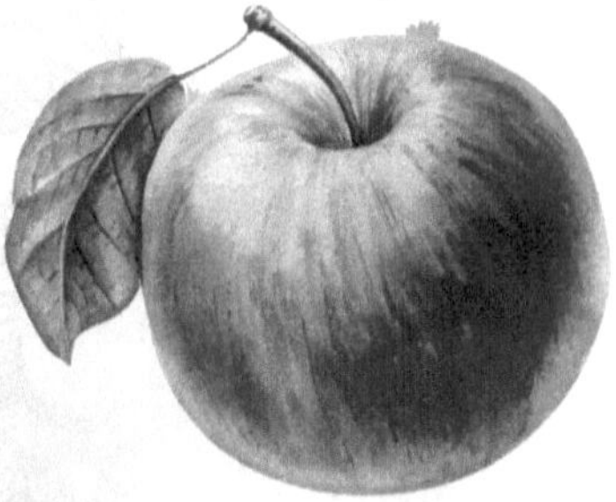

# AUTUMN

It was a busy Saturday and I was manning the store while Grandma took a break in the house to let the dog out. That was one of the perks about having your home be your work, too. It took about fifteen seconds to walk across the parking lot before you were on your front porch.

All morning long, I saw people I knew at the orchard, whether they were from Medina or just regular customers who came to the orchard every year.

Even as we made sales for apple picking and the other goodies that we had to offer at the store, in the back of my mind I couldn't help but remind myself that this was not enough. Grandma couldn't make enough

apple pies in the world to make up the amount of money we needed to be in good financial standing. And I was having my doubts that Braden's Apple Festival would be the saving grace that we had hoped it would be.

"Hey, there's my favorite apple-picker!" Micah Thomas said when he stepped up to the counter with his family.

I hadn't noticed them with all the other customers. "Hi, how are you guys?"

"Oh, just loading up on junk food." He glanced over his shoulder at his wife, who was following around their two kids—one was just over a year old, and the other was a very curious four-year-old who was touching everything he could get his hands on.

"Looks like your kids need more sugar, so you're in the right place." I began to ring out his things.

"I've been coming here since I was a kid," he said. "So has my wife. It's a shame our kids probably won't remember it."

"They will, over the years."

"Will they? I heard you're selling this place."

I stopped and looked up at him. "What?"

"Yeah. Well, that's what I *heard* at least." Based on my reaction, he was second-guessing his information.

"From who?"

"Uh...you know what? Never mind. I probably just heard it wrong."

"No, who told you that?" I didn't care how many people were in line. If rumors were circulating that I was selling the business, then all of our upcoming marketing attempts would be ruined, especially the Apple Festival. Maybe that was why we hadn't had as many vendors sign up as we'd hoped.

"Look, Autumn, I didn't mean to make you upset, I just—"

"Micah, please tell me where you heard that from." I locked eyes with him, refusing to let the topic go.

He looked back at his wife, then leaned in across the counter and lowered his voice. "There's a guy who's staying at the hotel who mentioned that he's here on business to buy this one."

"Braden," I said through clenched teeth.

Micah sighed and nodded. "Yeah, it was him. But look, he's been here for a month and you guys have been operating like normal, so I obviously misunderstood him."

My chest burned with betrayal and the store, the people, and everything around me seemed to fade away as I was very quickly consumed with my rage. How could I be so stupid to let Braden — the *enemy* — get so close to me? How could I not see it? He was working his way into our business to sabotage it. The Apple Festival was probably a ploy so that we would show the community that our once-mighty farm had truly fallen.

"Well, we are definitely *not* selling," I told Micah firmly. I finished ringing up his things and stuffed them into a bag, fuming.

I barely registered Micah's goodbye as he and his family left, and I was grateful when Grandma came back from her break, even if she did walk in with the backstabber, Braden Clinton, himself.

I stepped around the counter and maneuvered through the people in the shop, keeping my eyes on Braden.

"You! Come with me." What I wanted to do was slap him across the face, but my better judgment ruled out.

"Autumn, what's the matter?" Grandma asked.

I ignored her.

Without waiting for a reply from Braden, I led him across the parking lot and over to the front porch of the house, where we could talk in private.

Braden slowly stepped up the porch stairs, especially as I stood and crossed my arms and stared at him.

"Okay, you're clearly mad…"

"You're damn right I'm mad," I told him, forcing

myself to keep my voice hushed. The house had been hidden behind evergreen trees, but the sound still carried. "You're playing me."

"How am I playing you?"

I raised my eyebrows, blown away that he would deny the allegations when I had the proof on my side. "You're going around telling people that you're buying the farm, but then pretending that you're helping me try to keep it! Which is the truth? Oh, I know which one. The one that'll make you the most money."

"Whoa, Autumn, you have the wrong idea! I didn't say—" He stopped mid-sentence and hung his head. "You didn't, by chance, hear this from Micah, did you?"

"So what if I did?"

He sighed. "This is all just a big misunderstanding. I didn't mean to say that to him. I can talk to him and—"

"But you *did* say it, didn't you?"

He sighed. "Yes, but then my phone rang before I could explain anything else. It was actually a manager who called me. The band he represents agreed to come to the Apple Festival! The Running Dolls—have you heard of them?"

I kept my arms crossed and gritted my teeth.

"Okay, I guess not," he went on. "Anyway, now

that I have them booked, I can promote the band to vendors to sign up because a crowd draws a crowd, so if we can promise a big crowd we can—"

"There isn't a 'we,' Braden," I said. "In fact, I don't need your help anymore. With anything! I was running the farm just fine before you showed up." I bit back the rest of my words. We both knew what I said wasn't true. If I was running it fine, I wouldn't be facing the possibility of closure. "I just want you to leave."

"But—"

"Just go, Braden!" My voice carried louder than I intended. No doubt some people in the orchard heard me. Damn it.

He sucked in his lips and nodded. "Okay. I'll…uh, send you an email with everything I have worked on so far with the show. It's up to you if you want to continue to pursue it." He turned and walked down the path to our private driveway, where he had parked his car.

I watched until he pulled away, wrestling with myself whether I had made the right choice. But the fact remained, if I couldn't trust Braden, I couldn't work with him. Up until recently, the only ones who had been heavily involved with Chapman Farms had been family. Bringing someone else in had been a mistake.

Back in the country store, I stepped behind the counter, where Grandma was finishing up with a customer.

"What's the matter, dear?" she asked when she saw me. "Is everything okay? Where's Braden?"

"He won't be coming around here anymore," I said. "In fact, next time you see the hayride come around, tell them to put it away for the day. We're not doing that anymore. With the amount of gas that thing takes and how much it costs nowadays, it's a waste of money."

Grandma handed the bag to the customer and wished them a good day with a smile, then turned to me. "You're getting rid of the hayrides? But everyone loves them! They've been a big draw for people this year."

"They're going, Gram," I said firmly. "And a lot of the other changes we've made this year are going, too. This family has always run the orchard the same. There's no sense in switching things up."

"I think that's *exactly* the reason to switch things up."

"Well, you don't have a say in it, do you?" I scrunched my nose, knowing immediately just how much that had to hurt my grandmother. She had been perfectly understanding when, after Grandpa died, she found out that he had left the farm to only my dad and my uncles, even though she had been a major influence in the business over the course of their forty-year marriage. But I knew it still hurt her. And throwing it in her face wasn't fair.

"Gram…" I said, trying to apologize, but she had already escaped through the door behind the counter that led into our office.

Oh, the damage that had been done by Braden Clinton.

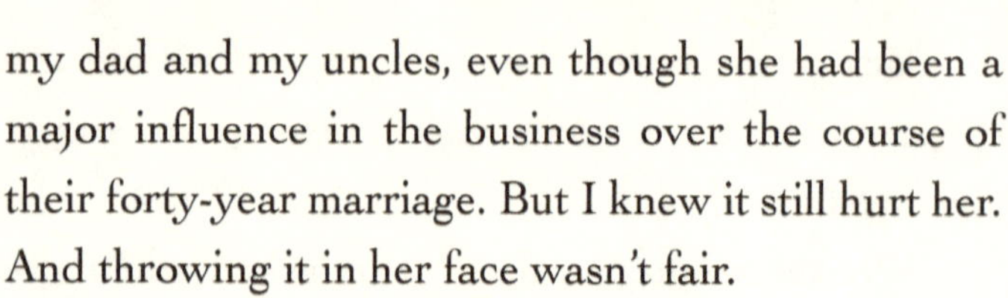

I couldn't sleep after everything that had happened. So I closed myself off in the office just off the store and fervently ran numbers over and over and over again, coming up with hypotheticals that would probably never happen, trying to figure out exactly how many apples we'd need to sell, how many baked goods, how many vendors we'd need so that we could make enough of a profit to turn things around for the farm.

I was certainly not an accountant and I kept screwing up the numbers. They never seemed to add up, especially the ones surrounding how much money was spent on the festival.

I switched over to the spreadsheet that Braden had sent me. He indicated a line for an "angel investor," but the way he had put it back when we first discussed finances with my uncles was that businesses would be investing in our festival, which would probably result in some kind of advertising. I saw no mention of ads in any of the documents he sent me.

So who was this angel investor? What kind of business wouldn't want their name plastered all over the marketing materials for an event like this?

Unless it wasn't a business.

I opened our bank account and scrolled back several weeks until I found the deposit from the angel investor. The entry noted the routing and account numbers and I copied them down onto a sticky note.

My next step in my private investigator work was to go to Google—where else?—and type in the routing number, which led me to the financial institution that it indicated.

Just as I suspected, it wasn't a formal bank. It was from a savings and loan association. Being that I was a farmer first and businesswoman second, I opened a new tab and Googled that same savings and loan association.

I read through the list of services and confirmed my thoughts. None of the ones listed included anything related to business. The money deposited in our account was from a personal account. And the

only one who had as much passion for this festival besides me was none other than Braden Clinton.

My anger with him only grew with that confirmation. But, we needed the money so I couldn't send it back. I was stuck, as much as I hated it. I would just have to put that money to good use so that we never had to rely on any "angel investors" again.

# Chapter Twenty
## AUTUMN

"All right, we'll see you in a couple weeks," I said into the phone. "Thank you for being a part of the Apple Festival! I'm looking forward to it."

Once I hung up, I squinted at my laptop screen, which I had propped open at the kitchen counter. Braden had sent over the spreadsheets he had created to keep track of the vendors. When he had first sent them, we only had about twenty people signed up. Since the Running Dolls had been confirmed and the article Sharon had done ran online, the number of vendors had jumped up to nearly a hundred—much higher than the fifty we had hoped for.

Over the last week, I had been taking calls about the

upcoming festival—Braden hadn't ended up using a fake name like he suggested, but instead pointed me out as the contact person—while Grandma had been reporting a significant uptick in foot traffic into the shop for U-Pick. Earlier this week, I had started cutting back on the number of apples we had available in the large wooden bins in the store, fearing that we'd run out before the last of them were ripe enough to pick and sell. And twice this week we had sold out of baked goods, which put me and Grandma baking more in the kitchen until late at night.

While that had been exhausting, it helped me and Grandma recover from our argument, and allowed me time to apologize. In true Grandma Wanda style, she waved it off and told us to shift our focus back to saving the orchard, which, thankfully, felt more like a reality now that interest in our farm had grown from the good press.

The oven timer beeped and Grandma came power-walking back into the kitchen, pumping her arms back and forth. "How are things looking?" She grabbed the oven mitts from the counter, slipped them on, then opened the oven door to peer inside. "Perfect."

"Hardly," I said. "We have so many things to manage for this event, in addition to the increased business, and have a staff of about five people to do it all. We're going to burn out before the festival even happens."

"We'll manage." Grandma set the pies she'd been baking on the stove, one-by-one. "We'll be exhausted, but we'll survive."

I sighed. "The thing is, I'm not sure we even *should* have this event. Is it even going to be successful? Braden's the one who had all the ideas and all the contacts, and I'm certainly *not* asking him for help again."

"What do you need his help for anymore?" Grandma leaned against the counter. "He's already helped more than any of us expected—and more than he should for someone working for our competitor."

"I'm not a businessperson like he is."

"Oh, please! I did not accept an invitation to a pity party, so you can cut that attitude out right now."

"Well, it's hard not to have that attitude when Braden lied to my face and I was dumb enough to believe him."

"I pushed you to get close to him," Grandma said. "And maybe I shouldn't have. But, if he fooled you with his charm, then he fooled me too. For what it's worth, though, I think his intentions were pure. I think he really *did* want to help us. Probably still does."

"Then why would he tell people that he's buying our farm?"

"Honey," she drew the word out, signifying that I needed to stop being so stubborn. As if Grandma was one to talk. "Think about it from his side. He works for Blossom Properties, who sent him here. Once he got to know us—got to know *you*—"

I rolled my eyes, but she pressed on.

"—he started to have a change of heart."

I had wondered that, too. And if Grandma was noticing the same thing, then there must be some ring of truth to it. But feelings had no place in business, right? Isn't that what Braden had taught me too?

"You'll never know how he really feels until you talk to him," Grandma said. "Maybe asking for help with—"

"I'm not asking for anymore help from him. And I'm *not* talking to him." Even I could hear the immaturity in my voice. But at the root of it, I was hurt that I had let Braden in to something so close to my heart—to our family's heart—and he had taken advantage of it.

"Be that as it may," Grandma pressed on. "I don't think it's a wise business decision to give up on this festival before it's even had a chance. It could be a huge boost for Chapman Farms, and you can't deny the effect it's already having on the business."

She came around the counter, kissed the top of my head and patted my shoulders, then retreated out of the room to tend to the next task on her to-do list for the evening.

The thought of her working so late at night at her age helped pull me out of my bull-headedness. I wanted the orchard to be successful. I wanted my family's legacy to continue on. But more than that, I wanted my grandma to truly be retired. And if using Braden's ideas got us enough cash flow to hire more people and take the workload off of my grandma, then that's what I was going to have to do.

# Chapter Twenty-One
## BRADEN

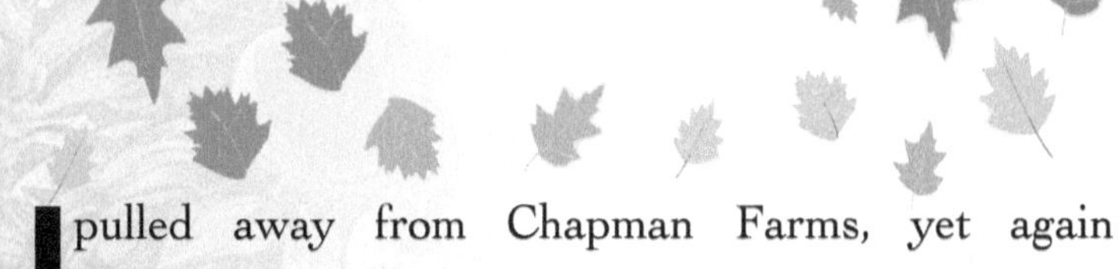

I pulled away from Chapman Farms, yet again unsuccessful in my attempts to talk to Autumn to patch things up. It was all just a misunderstanding, but I knew I'd been toeing the line, helping her while also keeping one foot in the door at Blossom Properties. I'd been stringing her along, and that wasn't fair.

She had every right to be mad at me.

This time, when I'd tried to talk to her just after closing, she hollered at me to get out. I didn't need her causing more of a scene that I knew we'd both regret, so I swallowed my pride and left.

I drove back to the hotel and walked up the steps to my room. My bag was already sitting at the end of the

bed, my clothes already packed. I only had a few last-minute things to gather up before I could finally return to my apartment and my life back in Buffalo.

As if that was what I wanted.

No, the trouble was, I wasn't sure *what* I wanted.

My involvement with Chapman Farms was officially over. With all the ignored phone calls and emails and texts, Autumn had made it abundantly clear that she wanted nothing more to do with me, so there was no sense in staying in Medina anymore. I would take a hit at work with Mr. Ramsey, sure. I would definitely lose out on that Director of Acquisitions title he'd promised me, but I'd get through it.

"Checking out early?" Micah asked somberly when I brought my bag down to the desk to check out.

"Yeah," I said with a sigh. "The Chapmans aren't selling. That's for sure."

"And it's a good thing they're not." He seemed to gain a newfound confidence in his perspective. Maybe word was spreading that the big bad city boy was coming in to try to take away their small town business, and people clearly had opinions about it. They certainly had a right to. "Chapman Farms is a staple here in Medina and they're not going anywhere."

"I certainly hope not."

Micah scrunched his eyebrows at first, then relaxed and nodded. "At least we agree on something."

"Anyway, thanks for accommodating me for such a long stay," I said. "I really did enjoy it here."

"Well, I'm…I'm glad." His determination to be mad at me seemed to conflict with his instinct to try to make me a repeat customer. People in small towns were protective of each other.

I went out to my car, tossed my bag in the backseat, and drove down Main Street, out of town. I had just barely passed the car dealership when I felt an overwhelming sense that I was making a mistake. But how could I argue with someone who wouldn't even talk to me?

At the red light, I pulled out my phone and hit the one person on my speed dial who I knew would take my call.

"Hello?"

"Hey, Len."

"Brady! What's up?"

I sighed. "Oh, I don't know. I'm heading back home."

"As in, *home* home?"

"Yes, my apartment. I checked out of the hotel room in Medina today."

"Big move," he said. "You've been there so long I thought you'd be moving to Medina here soon enough."

I laughed, although the truth was, I could see it. Being that my profession was in business, the possibility of calling a small town like Medina home seemed like too far of a reality, but now that I'd spent some time essentially advising Autumn and Chapman Farms, I definitely felt like it was a better fit for my personality.

"How're you doing?" Lenny asked after my silence.

"I don't know. Not great, I guess."

"Is it that girl?"

"There was nothing going on with us. Not really. Not like I thought."

Lenny was quiet for a moment, then, "I'm sorry to hear that. Really. It was nice to see you moving on with your life."

"Moving on from your sister?"

"Sara will never truly be gone, Brady," he said. "There's too many memories. But the fact is, she died. We need to continue to live our lives. You especially."

I took in a deep breath, trying to digest the reality of his words.

"Look at it this way, you made your first attempt to move on from Sara. And, okay, it didn't work out.

But now that you've tried it, you'll be much better suited to do it again."

"Yeah, maybe."

"You might not feel like it now, but this fling you had with this girl was probably a really good thing for you."

I scoffed. No, it certainly didn't feel like it at all.

The rest of the car ride was quiet as I drove back to my apartment in the increasing darkness. By the time I parked my car in the complex and walked the familiar path back to my specific apartment building, the sky was almost completely dark, which was drowned out by the strength of the super-bright white LED overhead lights shining over the parking lot. Not a star in sight.

When I let myself in my apartment, I flicked on the lights and dropped my bag on the couch from behind. My body worked on autopilot as I stepped through the familiar one-bedroom apartment that I had once shared with my wife. This time, though, something was off.

Sure, the air was stale, and the mail was piling up, and the whole place could've used a good vacuuming and certainly a dusting, but there was something else to the weirdness I was feeling. Maybe it was just that I hadn't been back to the apartment in the nighttime in almost a month.

I grabbed a beer from the fridge—luckily that hadn't expired—and plopped down on the couch. There was a good chance that was where I'd be for the rest of the night now that I'd sat down, but that was okay. I didn't have the energy for much else.

I sipped my beer and tried to relax, and that was when I realized what exactly had changed: me. This apartment, which had once brought so much comfort, especially in the days immediately following Sara's passing, no longer felt like home. I felt like I was visiting someplace else and that my heart belonged back in Medina.

Of course, I didn't actually belong in Medina, either. As it was, I didn't belong anywhere.

# Chapter Twenty-Two
## AUTUMN

The night before the first Apple Festival was a lot more hectic than I had originally thought it would be. I knew there'd be fires to put out, but coordinating all the vendor arrivals while others set up, at the same time other questions were asked almost incessantly, *and* while a seemingly endless amount of baskets were being dropped off for the Chinese auction—it was all very overwhelming.

"I requested electricity!"

"I'm right next to a woman who also makes dog sweaters!"

"Will there be overnight security?"

"Is it too late to sign up to become a vendor?"

"Can I move my spot?"

I had already traveled up and down the main aisle of the orchard at least a hundred times. The familiar farm, which I had known like the back of my hand my whole life, had taken on a new perspective as pop-up canopies of various shapes, sizes, and colors began to line the grassy row, creating a makeshift Main Street.

Once the final vendors had pulled in for the night before set-up, I made my way back down the main pathway toward the country store. I checked in with vendors as I passed, making sure everyone was satisfied with what they needed, and writing down whatever else was requested of me.

"Sammy, can you get the guy selling the metal bookshelves a screwdriver?" I asked once I finally made my way back to the country store, where Grandma Wanda was standing next to him with a clipboard. "He forgot one and he needs it to tighten his stand so that it doesn't topple over onto people."

"Sure thing." He set off to find one.

I took a deep breath—probably my fortieth in the last fifteen minutes alone—and looked to the sky. There was a gentle breeze, which brought the chilly fall air that hinted at winter, but it wasn't enough to cause any damage to any of the vendors' tents.

"Looks like we're going to have nice weather for it," Grandma said.

"Mm-hmm." The weather forecast had said there was a slight chance of rain for Sunday, but another report said it could possibly hit late Saturday night. The show technically ended at five on Saturday, so I figured that everyone would be out by seven or eight at the latest—vendors included. It would be dark by then, but we could set up some floodlights to help people see as they packed up. I just hoped the rain held off that long.

"Have you confirmed with the food trucks?"

I nodded. "Yeah."

"And you measured to make sure they'd fit in the parking lot?"

"It'll be tight, but it should be fine. The plan is to have them park just on the other side of the fence by the parking lot, so the fumes and noise from their engines don't bother anyone at the festival."

"Wouldn't it be better to put them at the end of the row?" Grandma used her pen to indicate in the direction she was talking about, at the end of the main pathway where the vendors were all lined up and where the perpendicular main path cut through and formed a *T*.

I shook my head. "No, because they wouldn't be able to get in or out until the pathway was clear, and

with all these vendors coordinating, that would take a while. Besides, I don't want anyone to get stuck if it starts raining and gets muddy." Another deep breath as I surveyed the vendors all setting up their booths.

"What about the band?"

"They're going on the end, but I figured their van will be able to make it down the tractor path," I said. "If all else fails, we can load up their equipment on one of our trailers."

"Isn't that going to be used for hayrides?"

I sighed. "I'm not sure we'll be able to do hayrides."

"But you promoted it on the flyer."

"I know, but we ended up getting way more vendors than I expected, which pushed the show toward that back path more." I shook my head. "I hope people aren't disappointed."

"Maybe we can pull out one of the smaller tractors, then."

"But we don't have a trailer that fits that tractor with seats on it," I countered. "It's too late, Gram. No hayrides."

"I think you're making a mistake."

I stomped my foot and huffed. "Then *you* plan all of this!"

Grandma smiled and latched her arm around me

for a tight sideways hug. "I know you're stressed out, honey, but you need to relax! You've got some good instincts, so I'll trust them."

"Hopefully those instincts are right."

"Even if they're not, we'll learn for next year."

"*If* we have a next year."

"Don't talk like that," Grandma said. "This show is already a huge success! The hard part is done. The interest is there. Everyone I've talked to has said they're coming. Tomorrow, I just want you to enjoy yourself and be the boss that you are." She leaned over and kissed my cheek. "I'm proud of you."

That brought a smile to my face despite myself. "Thanks, although I'm not sure I should accept it. A lot of the organizing that went into all of this was Braden's doing."

He's the one who made the calls, who set up the insurance, and who implemented the marketing plan. By the time it fell in my lap, a lot of the bigger parts of putting the show together had already been done. All I had done was make sure that those plans were followed.

"Nonsense," Grandma said. "Don't discredit your work."

I took in another deep breath as my phone buzzed with a text. It was from Percy Langston, the band manager for the Running Dolls. He wanted me to call him. Probably to confirm the details for tomorrow.

I groaned. "Here I go again, on another phone call."

"Why don't you call Braden and ask him for help?"

"Nope." I typed out a text back to Percy. "Not going there."

"Autumn…"

"Grandma, look. I know he helped. I know he did a lot of work. And I know I'm stressed, but I'm *not* going to call our competitors for help just because I'm a little stressed out. It's our *family* business and, last I checked, he's *not* our family."

"Not yet."

"Not *ever*. He's made it clear that all he wants to do is take our business from us and I have no intention of letting him do that."

I took another survey of the vendors setting up and decided to take the momentary reprieve to make the call to Percy.

"I really don't think that's what he wants," Grandma said.

"I have to call the band manager," I told her. "I'll be back in a second. Can we just drop this whole Braden thing?"

Grandma shrugged. "If you say so."

"Oh, and if you're looking to help, can you find a good place for the Chinese auction baskets to go? We got a lot more than I thought."

Grandma nodded. "I'll take care if it, dear. Don't you worry about it."

"Thank you."

Still feeling overwhelmed—and a little unsettled—I escaped into the store to make the phone call to Percy. I could do this on my own. I didn't need anyone's help. Especially not from Braden.

# Chapter Twenty-Three
## AUTUMN

It was hard to believe that it was already the day of the Apple Festival. For better or worse, all of the efforts over the last month or so would be put to the test.

I wasn't sure I was ready for it.

I woke up before the sun, as always. The mid-October chill in the morning air brought a serious nip, so I donned a thicker sweatshirt and headed out to inspect the vendors' tents. I wanted to make sure nothing bad had happened overnight. If anything did happen, I wanted to call those vendors ahead of time so they were prepared for what they were coming into.

Luckily, after my walk through the orchard, I spotted nothing amiss other than heavy dew. Grandma had set

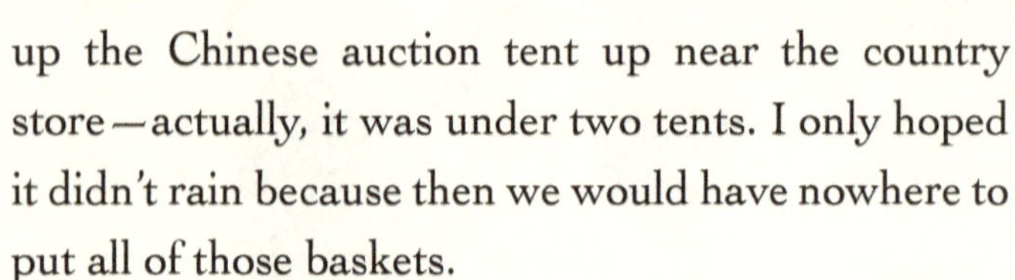

up the Chinese auction tent up near the country store—actually, it was under two tents. I only hoped it didn't rain because then we would have nowhere to put all of those baskets.

Satisfied that things were shaping up, I went out to the barn and fired up the tractor that had already been loaded up with the trailer, just in case the band needed it to transfer their equipment. Judging by the way the weather was turning out, I didn't think we'd need it.

I loaded up the trash cans onto the trailer and drove down the main aisle, depositing the cans along the way. By the time I pulled the tractor back into the barn, some of the vendors had already started arriving, including Hattie, who had set up a coffee stand right by the country store, signifying the start to the row of vendors.

"Here you go!" She handed me a to-go cup.

"What do I owe you?"

"Nothing."

"Hattie…"

"Autumn, seriously! I'm really proud of you and all the work you've done for this Apple Festival. People have been talking about it in the shop for weeks. I'm just glad I get to be a part of it."

"Considering you're a former employee, I don't see why I *wouldn't* invite you."

She smiled. "Brings me back to the days on the farm."

I laughed, then held up the cup. "You really don't want anything for this?"

She waved it off. "Nah. I just made myself a complimentary cup. Besides, consider it my gift to you for a job well done."

"We'll see."

"Hey, no matter what happens today, you've brought the conversation back to Chapman Farms, and that's important."

I gave her a hesitant smile. "Thanks. And thanks for this." I held up the drink, then started making my way down the row of vendors to check in with them.

The festival officially started at ten o'clock, so naturally by ten-oh-five, I was already panicking that we would have a bad turn out.

"Would you relax?" Grandma said as another family passed through the country store on the way to the festival.

We had taken Braden's suggestion and had decided to offer everyone a small complimentary bag for them to pick apples before they even got to the main part of the festival. A lot of people took that as

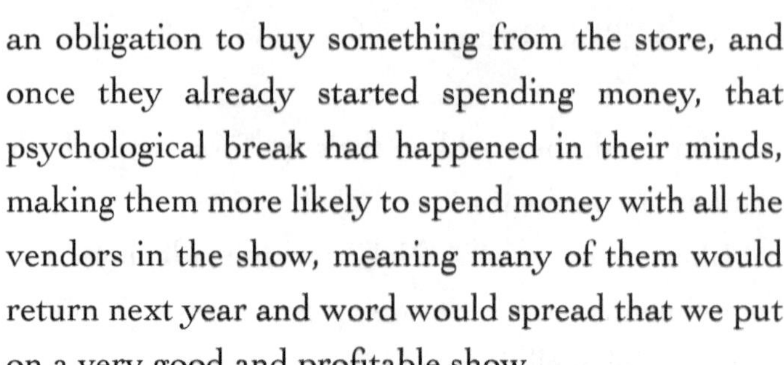





an obligation to buy something from the store, and once they already started spending money, that psychological break had happened in their minds, making them more likely to spend money with all the vendors in the show, meaning many of them would return next year and word would spread that we put on a very good and profitable show.

That was the theory, at least.

"How many have we had so far?" I tried to glance out the door to count the number of cars in the parking lot, but the next family coming in had to wait in line and were blocking my view.

"It doesn't matter." Grandma took the change from the next person in line as they paid for a muffin. "Your job today is to relax."

"Can't. I'm working."

"Autumn Chapman, look what you've done!"

I turned and saw Sharon, the reporter from the online newspaper, step inside. She had a camera hung from her neck.

I smiled at her. "It's turned out well so far, hasn't it?"

Sharon's eyes went wide. "Are you *kidding*? There's a line out the door and there are cars all over the parking lot and the road out front! Autumn, you're bringing in the crowd!"

I couldn't help but smile at that. It was nice to get

validation from someone outside of the family.

"Excuse me," one of the customers said as she tried to get to the shelf Sharon and I were standing in front of.

We scooted to the side to allow her room.

"I'm going to head out and take some pictures," Sharon told me. "Maybe we can meet up later, once things have calmed down a little, for an interview."

I smiled again. "I'd love that. Thank you!" Meanwhile, I wondered if there was enough of a crowd outside to make the photos look like the Apple Festival was worth coming to. But, there was nothing more I could do.

I decided to take another lap around the festival to make sure all the vendors had what they needed. Better to be over-attentive than absent.

The sun had come out and the air was warmer, so I pulled off my sweatshirt, leaving a red flannel underneath. If I stayed in the sun, I was warm. In the shade, I was cold. The joys of fall in Western New York.

From down at the end of the aisle, I could hear the band start their soundcheck, so I pressed on in that direction. The Running Dolls were going on at twelve noon, so they had a narrow timeline in order to get any issues cleared up. Halfway down the main aisle, I stopped when I heard my name.

I spun on my heels, recognizing the voice but not being able to place it with all the other distractions.

But there was no missing that powder-blue dress shirt.

"Seriously?" I said. "That's what you wear to the Apple Festival?"

Braden picked at his shirt and looked down at it, then smiled at me. "I wasn't going to, but I knew how much you liked it, so I made sure to wear it today."

Luckily, what chill that was left in the air helped hide my reddening cheeks. Still, I smiled at him.

He took a step closer, but I put up my hands and took a half-step back. I was still upset with him. If he had it his way, the orchard would be gone and would become an empty soulless landscape, like so many other family farms before ours.

"I didn't think you'd come," I said. That was safe. That was neutral.

"I wasn't planning on it," he admitted. "I didn't think you'd want me here."

"So why did you?"

"Because I wanted to see you."

Another smile. It was like I didn't have control over my own body around him.

"It's also hard to turn down a personal invitation from Wanda," he added.

I scoffed and rolled my eyes. "Of course she

called you."

"Yeah. I figured you probably had no idea about that call."

I noticed more people filling into the main aisle as the crowd thickened. Side conversations began happening between vendors and customers, but Braden and I were in our own world at the moment.

"What did your boss say when you lost the account?" I asked.

"He was disappointed, but I convinced him that Chapman Farms wasn't as fragile of a business as he thought."

"So I take it he doesn't know you're here?"

"Nope. But I don't need his approval anyway."

I hooked an eyebrow. "You do if you want to keep your job. I would think that losing our account would put you on thin ice with him."

"That's the thing, though. I don't want to keep my job."

I was confused. "What?"

"I quit my job at Blossom Properties."

I stared at him, clearly not hearing him correctly, and waited for the smile to crack on his face to show that he was joking.

But he remained serious, almost taking on a concerned look.

"Autumn?"

"You *quit*?"

"Yes."

"Why?"

He shrugged. "I guess I realized that I overstayed my welcome there. I no longer needed that type of job."

"But…you were making so much money."

"I know. But that doesn't matter as much to me anymore. I have a lot stashed away in savings. I'll be okay for a little bit."

I looked down at our feet in the matted grass. They had somehow grown closer. *We* had somehow grown closer. "I know you were the investor that gave money to us for this Apple Festival."

He nodded. "Uh-huh." He said it so matter-of-factly, as if it wasn't of any issue at all that he had given thousands to a company that he had been tasked with buying.

But that was when he worked for Blossom Properties—and had the salary of someone who worked there—and he no longer had either.

"Why would you give up all that money?"

"I believe in Chapman Farms. I believe in *you*, Autumn. The passion you have for this place, the history it has, the sense of community behind it…that combination is something that I've never seen with any of our other accounts at Blossom Properties.

Here, the orchard isn't just another line item on a budget, but the heart and soul of your family and a cornerstone in this community. *That's* what I'm drawn to, not a fat wallet."

I tilted my head to the side and raised my eyebrows. "I would like a fat wallet."

He brought a finger to my chin and lifted my head up toward him. "But you wouldn't trade your soul in order to have it. Because of that, I knew you wouldn't accept it if I tried to give you a check. So funneling money into this event was the best way that I could help you without any hard feelings."

My insides burned as I felt Braden looking directly into *my* soul. My heart. It was like he held it right in his hands.

He pulled his hand away and smiled. "I have to say, though, I am relieved now that I've officially quit. I only took the job at Blossom Properties to help pay for Sara's medical bills, and quitting feels like I've returned to myself again. Like I'm back on track to where I was heading before Sara's medical stuff necessitated changes."

"But now you're unemployed. What are you going to do? You can't live on savings forever."

"Well, I was *hoping* a local apple orchard might be looking for a business manager…"

I caught on to his line of thinking and smirked at

him. "We're actually looking more for a jack of all trades and I'm not sure you fit the bill."

He chuckled. "Are you kidding? I'm pretty sure I've excelled at everything we've done together."

"I don't know. You haven't won over Maggie yet."

He gave an exaggerated eye roll. "Please! One little dog."

"I don't know. She's important to Grandma, and if you can't win over the dog, then you can't win over Grandma, and if you don't win over Grandma—"

"Your grandmother has gotten me to take off my shirt for her, so I think I've won her over."

I shook my head, loving the easy back-and-forth we'd fallen into again. "I don't know. My grandma doesn't impress easy."

Braden moved closer to me, talking softer now, forcing me to lean in so I could hear him over the gathering crowd that had filtered in to the orchard at some point while we were talking. "Considering that she gave me a personal invitation here, I think she likes me. And I think you like me too."

"What makes you say that?" I asked.

He responded with a kiss pressed gently to my lips, then proceeded to wrap his arms around me and squeeze my body tight as we both leaned into it. I felt all the stress from the show, from the orchard, from the business—all of it—wash away from my body. In the moment, pressed against Braden, I felt at peace. At home.

Finally, he pulled away, and I suddenly felt all eyes on me, which caused my face to go as red as the apples on the trees surrounding us. Braden noticed and took my hand and led me through the small space between vendor tents and down one of the rows of trees that had been picked over for the season already. Our tiny bit of privacy as more and more people came to visit Chapman Farms.

"So, not to state the obvious or anything, but where do things stand between us?" I asked. "If we're going to work together and…*other things*…then we need to establish where the boundaries are."

"Well…" Braden swung my arm as our hands remained locked together and we wandered down the row. "I like you, and you like me, and judging by that very public display of affection, I think it'd be more of a pain in the butt answering all those questions about us if we *didn't* see where things went between us."

I rolled my eyes. "So this is only a publicity stunt?"

He stopped and turned to me, running a hand along my cheek. "What do you think?"

I felt the electricity flow through my body again.

There was *definitely* something here that was more than just publicity. Truth be told, now that he was with with me, I had missed him. A lot. "You know, we drive each other nuts."

He shrugged. "So? What couple doesn't?"

*Couple.* That word put a permanency on this *thing* between us that I hadn't associated with us before.

"Are you sure you're ready to be a couple with someone else?" I asked carefully. "Someone other than Sara?"

He took in a deep breath. "Sara will always be a part of me. But she's a part of my past—a very important part, sure, but a part of my past nonetheless. I'm ready to start living for my future. Whatever that looks like."

I smiled. "It kills you not to have a plan, doesn't it?"

He made a face. "Just a little." He squeezed my hand a little tighter. "But I'm in good hands."

"Can we agree on something before we move any further?"

"Sure."

"Can we please stop with the corny lines?"

He threw his head back and dropped his shoulders. "Yes!" He released my hand and put his arm around me instead as we headed back to the

festival. "I will say this, though, I really do think Sara would've liked you."

I smiled and leaned into him. Even though I'd never met Sara, it was nice to know that, in a way, I had her blessing.

# Chapter Twenty-Four
## BRADEN

The Apple Festival really was a sight to behold. It was amazing to see the orchard filled with all kinds of people from the community and beyond. I recognized many of the vendors, who I'd been in contact with before handing over the reigns to Autumn, as well as other people from out toward Buffalo who had come to Medina to visit.

"I never knew this was here! How cute!" one woman said as she passed by us.

"We'll have to come back next year," another one said.

Most of all, I was proud of Autumn for completely taking over the organization of the festival and making it all her own.

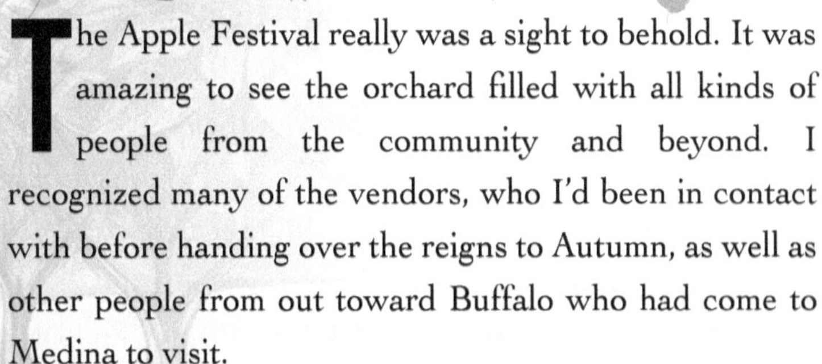

Autumn went to check in with the Running Dolls as they set up. They were scheduled to go on at noon and it was almost that time.

While she met with each band member, I stood by with Percy.

"Thank you for taking a chance with this festival," I told him. "It means a lot to me — to us — and it really did make a difference for the show."

Percy smiled. "Looks like it's a good show. Are you making this an annual thing?"

I pointed over to Autumn, who was on stage talking with the drummer. She had her notepad out, so she was probably taking his lunch order.

"You'd have to ask the boss," I told him. "But I think that's the plan."

"Well, count us in for next year, then."

As Autumn came down the stairs, Percy slapped me on the shoulder and told me to take care.

"I figured a complimentary lunch is good," she said as we power-walked back down the main aisle. "That's good, right? I mean, we're paying them, but we could also offer them lunch, right?"

"Yeah, that's fine."

"Okay."

Back at the hot dog stand, which was halfway down the row of vendors, Autumn went to get in line to put in the orders for the band. As we parted, I saw

a familiar face that threw me off since I was seeing him in a different environment.

Lenny came in for a hug and it wasn't until he had wrapped his arms around me that it fully registered that he was standing in front of me. Bernie and the kids walked up behind him.

"Hey, nice to see you!" Lenny said after we parted.

I stood in shock. "How did you—I'm surprised you came!"

"You've been talking about working with this place for a while now. I thought it'd be worth our while to take a little road trip up here."

"It's beautiful up here," Bernie said.

"Can we go back and get a cider donut?" my nephew Henry asked.

"Yeah, Mom! Can we?" Eva, my niece, echoed.

Bernie looked to Lenny to be the bad guy and he deflected to me.

"They *are* good…"

Bernie shot me a look. "Okay. Fine. But only one each!" She looked to her husband. "Do you want any?"

"They're *good*," I taunted.

Lenny relented. "Yeah, you might as well. Just one, though." After Bernie and the kids wandered off, he turned back to me and murmured, "We're

going to bring home enough junk today…"

I smiled and spread my arms wide, indicating the festival. "That's what all of this is about."

"Yeah, this is impressive," he said. "Congratulations on the festival."

"It wasn't my doing." I gestured to Autumn, who was walking back from the hot dog stand with several to-go boxes stacked high. "It was all her."

"What was me?" she asked.

"Putting together the Apple Festival."

"Oh. Yeah. Well, sort of. Braden helped. *A lot.*"

"I'm Lenny," he said.

"Autumn."

"I'd introduce you to my wife and kids, but your apple cider donuts have tempted them away," Lenny said with a smile.

"How old are they?" she asked.

"My son just turned six and my daughter is three."

Autumn smiled. "My cousins are running around here somewhere. They're a bit older than that. My youngest cousin is eight and my oldest is twelve, but I'm sure they'd have no issues with your kids tagging along." She looked around the corner and saw a small kid running down the row of apple trees. She smiled again. "Looks like they picked up the same hobby that I had when I was a kid: running through the orchard."

"That's good! My kids are kind of shy, but maybe I can get them to join them," Lenny said. "After all this sugar, we're going to need them to crash."

Autumn laughed and when the moment passed, she said, "I'm sorry, but do I know you from somewhere, or are you a customer or…?"

"Lenny's my—" I spoke up quickly, but got caught up on what to refer to him as. "—He's Sara's brother."

Autumn nodded with recognition on her face.

Lenny extended his hand, but withdrew it when he noticed that both of Autumn's were full with the to-go boxes.

She smiled. "Well, it was nice to meet you. I'll shake your hand later."

He laughed. "Sounds good."

"All right, I need to go run these to the band before they go on. I don't want them starving the whole time they're up there." She hurried off down the aisle back toward the stage.

"So I take it that's the girl you were talking about?" Lenny asked after she had left.

I didn't know exactly what Autumn and I were to each other, besides the ambiguous "seeing where things were going." At the same time, though, I

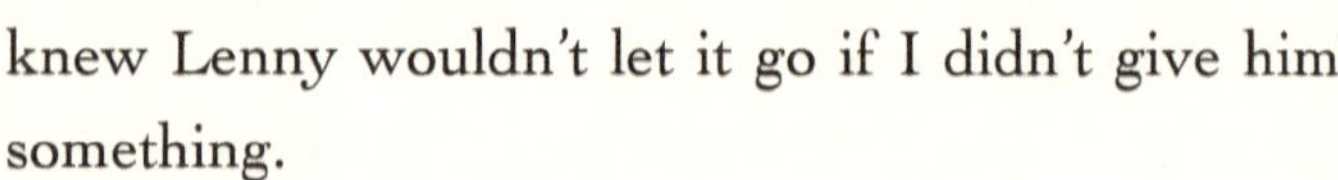

knew Lenny wouldn't let it go if I didn't give him something.

So I glanced over at him and gave him a wink. That was about all I would say on the subject at the moment.

# AUTUMN

After the festival was over, after all the vendors had cleaned up, and after all the trash was put in the dumpster and the orchard had been returned to a semi-normal state, I sat at the dining room table surrounded by Braden, Grandma, Uncle Stan, and Uncle Jim. Piles of money lay in front of us, separated by their denominations as Braden counted it out.

"So how did we do?" I asked quietly.

"I won't have solid answers to that until I weigh it against the expenses, but as long as you kept control over your spending, I think you're looking at a very sizable profit."

I sighed and relaxed into my chair. I was exhausted to the point where I felt a little drunk. My phone said I had walked over twenty thousand steps, and I thought that was a massive understatement.

"So you think we can keep the farm?" Grandma asked.

Braden passed the paper he'd been recording the revenue on over to Uncle Stan. "Like I said, I'd have to really dig into the numbers to give you a solid answer, but I think it's likely."

"*This* is how much we made?" Uncle Stan was surprised.

"I've been hearing people talking about the orchard and today's Apple Festival for a few weeks now," Uncle Jim added. "I think, if nothing else, this has really helped us advertise the business."

Grandma nodded. "I talked to several people today who said they knew others who wanted to come but couldn't make it because we turned this around on such short notice. I think next year, we'll get an even bigger turnout."

My eyes grew wide. Next year? Bigger? I was going to need more help.

"I think that if we can recreate this, we can swing keeping the farm open," Uncle Stan said. "But I have to admit, relying on one weekend in the fourth quarter of the year for the profitability of our business doesn't leave me with a lot of hope for the future. I don't want to leave the success of the business each year up to something as fickle as the weather."

And just like that, my buzz deflated a little.

Braden nodded. "I've thought about that."

Of course he had.

"And I have some ideas for how to increase profitability throughout the year," Braden went on. "Ideas that align within your business model and your family's morals. I know that's important to you all."

Uncle Jim nudged me, which perked me up as sleep had begun to win the fight. "He should be working for us."

My eyes flittered over to Braden, who smirked. It had been an unofficial agreement between us that he would be hired by Chapman Farms. The exact details of that hadn't quite been worked out yet, though, nor would they until at *least* Monday.

Instead, I looked over at Uncle Jim and simply said, "We'll talk."

"What about the vendors?" Grandma asked. "How did they do?"

"Oh! I don't even know. I haven't been on my phone really all day." I pulled it out and saw the flood of emails in my inbox from vendors.

"You know, if the vendors aren't happy and don't come again, then our show suffers and people stop coming and then we're right back where we were," Grandma went on.

Just by scanning the previews and subject lines of each message, I could tell that we wouldn't have that issue again. In fact, it looked like I had some emails from new vendors who wanted to be added to a list about next year's show.

"By the looks of it, everyone was really happy with the show," I reported.

"And we're being tagged in a lot of Facebook posts," Uncle Jim said from beside me as he scanned his own phone through his reading glasses.

"Make sure we reply positively to all of them," Braden said. "And not just some standard copy-and-paste message, either. These responses need to be personalized. I know it'll take a while, but this is how we further cement ourselves in the community and create a culture that makes people *care* about what we're doing."

His use of the word "we" sparked a fire in me that I didn't ever think a two-letter word would.

Uncle Stan looked over at me, then at Uncle Jim before turning back to Braden. "I know I'm probably stating the obvious at this point, but I think it's safe to say that we're not going to sell our business to Blossom Properties. At least, not at this point in time. Hopefully never."

Braden smiled. "I'm so glad to hear that, but you'll have to let Blossom Properties know. As of

yesterday, I no longer work there."

"You don't?" There was hope in Grandma's voice.

"Nope." He shook his head.

"He works for us now," I said proudly.

"Oh, good!" Grandma cheered.

"What is it, exactly, that he'll be doing?" Uncle Jim asked me.

"We still need to work that out," I admitted.

Braden looked at me as another smile spread across his face. "I have some ideas."

# Epilogue:
## One Year Later
### AUTUMN

The second annual Apple Festival had been easier to plan and market. Not only because we had more time to do it all, but also because we had the success from the first festival to rely on.

Plus, this time around, I had Braden to help, who had been a godsend over the last year because he'd been able to fully take the reigns on the business's finances and help steer us in the right direction toward profitability.

I carried to-go containers filled with food down to one of the stages to give to the next band to go on. This year, we'd been able to get enough buzz to book bands for most of the day, requiring two different stages so

each band could set up and take down while another one played.

"Here we go," I said as I stepped underneath their canopy beside the stage, where they had set up their merch table. "We have the grilled cheese, we have the turkey club, the tacos, chicken fingers, and a hot dog with fries."

Not only had we been able to recruit more bands for this year, but we'd had more interest from people who owned food trucks, who wanted to be a part of our festival. So now instead of just a hot dog stand run by the local Kiwanis Club, we also had a slew of other options for food, which not only helped draw the crowd, but kept them at the festival.

"Thank you," one of the band members said. He had long hair and was sporting a sleeveless T-shirt that showed off his tattoo sleeves, despite the fifty-degree weather. "What do we owe you?"

I put up my hands. "Don't worry about it. It's on us. Consider this a thank you for supporting us."

"Of course! When our buddies with the Running Dolls told us how cool the show was last year, we knew we wanted to be a part of it this year."

"Well, I appreciate it," I said. "If you need anything else, you have my number." I bid them goodbye, then started off back down the main aisle, which was packed with a crowd and lined with tents for vendors.

We'd had so much interest from vendors that we had to move the stages down the other main aisle that ran adjacent to the one coming from the country store. Based on the number of people who had asked where the stage was, I wasn't sold that that was the best place for them, but that was where we had committed to for this year, so we had to make do. We'd have to consider another placement for next year.

"Hey there, beautiful." Braden's voice cut through the crowd before I even laid eyes on him through the throng.

When my eyes finally settled on him, I smiled and reached for his arm. "Hey! I just brought lunch to the next band, University Files, and then I'm going to go check in on Grandma."

"Just did," he said. "Her book is selling almost as fast as her pies."

Apparently, Grandma had been secretly writing a cookbook last year while I was trying to save the orchard. After the Apple Festival, she announced that she had finished, then hooked up with a local printing company to have it printed and worked with the local library and the bookstore on Main Street to

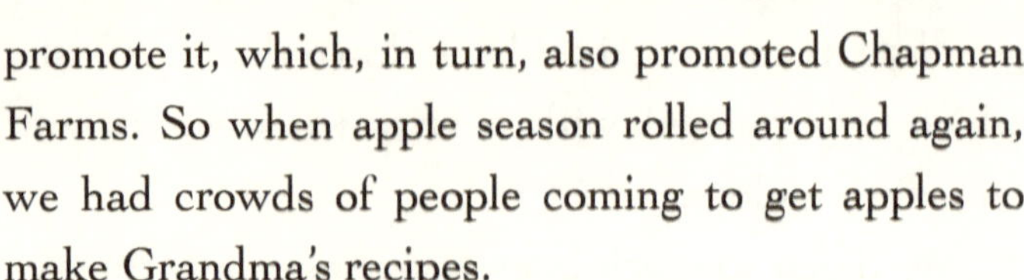



promote it, which, in turn, also promoted Chapman Farms. So when apple season rolled around again, we had crowds of people coming to get apples to make Grandma's recipes.

I smiled at Braden. "Good. How's the parking situation looking?"

"It's flowing as smoothly as can be expected," he said. "The kids are doing a great job keeping things flowing into the field. I'm not sure people particularly *like* having to walk so far, but judging by the crowd, I think everyone has considered the walk worth it."

Another thing we modified for this year: working with the couple who owned the field across the street from our farm so we could use it for parking for the event. That left our regular parking lot strictly for handicap parking.

"Good," I said. "Maybe next year we can plan a shuttle or something."

"More costs."

"But it'll be worth it," I said. "If anything comes up with the parking situation this year, let me know."

"I can handle it, too," he said. "You need to relax and enjoy the show."

I shook my head. "I'm *working* the show."

He squeezed my hands. "But you also need to enjoy it." He gave me a quick kiss, then nodded off toward one of the vendor tents. "I have to go.

Apparently one of the tents keeps getting caught in the breeze and it's about to blow away."

"Stakes are in the—"

He pulled several stakes out of his pocket—his *jeans* pocket. He had been dressing more casually now that he was officially a part of the Chapman Farms team. He still wore a dress shirt most days, including today under his sweater, but it was nice to see him finally letting loose a little.

"Already got them," he said. "I'll see you later?"

"Definitely."

I made my way to the country store, where Grandma was signing another book and talking to a group of women who seemed enraptured by her tales. The genuine smiles on all of their faces brought one to mine.

Beside Grandma, Emma was busy cashing out the next person in line, which wrapped around the store. Emma was one of our newest recruits, having just joined the team last month at the start of the school year.

Braden had had the idea to partner with the agricultural program that I went through in high school to offer hands-on experience to students. That meant I was doing more teaching in the orchard more days than I would like, but the extra help was nice. Many of the students had been hired part-time to

work weekends for us in addition to their time at the farm during school hours.

I went out to the parking lot to check on the traffic flow and at the edge of the parking lot, right at the line of construction fencing, I spotted Uncle Stan and Uncle Jim admiring the work being done on the house.

Some of the privacy trees had been cut down to reveal the back portion of the house that had been under construction for the last few months. Most of the work inside had been completed and, in fact, a lot of the landscape and outside finishing work was supposed to be done in time for the Apple Festival, but delays happened and so now they were scheduled to finish up by the end of the month.

We had decided to tackle the house first, and later the barn based on a number of factors. First was the cost. We needed the income from the rentals in order to further financially support the renovation of the barn. And second, the buzz we had gotten from the Apple Festival last year made it obvious that people wanted to "retreat" to the orchard and were looking for unique and rural places to stay to escape the chaos of their lives.

"What do you think?" I asked as I walked up to them. I nodded toward the house to indicate what I was talking about.

"Very nice." Uncle Jim put his arm around my shoulders when I walked up.

"Looks like there's still a lot of work to be done," Uncle Stan said.

I shrugged. "Maybe, but they say it'll be done soon. As long as the weather holds up, they're going to pour the concrete for the sidewalk on Monday. Then once that sets, they'll do landscaping and then it's pretty much done."

The project had converted the back addition of the house into essentially micro townhomes. There were four of them in total, both occupying upstairs and downstairs. We figured they'd mostly be booked by the wedding party once the barn event space was finished, so one for the bride and groom, one for the groom's parents, one for the bride's parents, and one for the wedding party. They were small, but comfortable.

"Do you want to see inside?" I offered.

Uncle Jim shook his head. "No. I don't want to track in any unnecessary mud. We can wait until they finish up."

"Are they staying on budget?" Uncle Stan asked.

I nodded. "Yup. Braden's been keeping on top of that." I turned and pointed to the barn beside us. The one with the iconic Chapman Farms sign. "In

fact, he's already started getting some quotes on the work for the barn."

"Any ideas on the costs for that?" Uncle Stan asked.

"Not sure yet," I admitted. "They're still determining the scope of work that needs to be done. But we do already have a few bookings for the townhomes, once they're done. A few people are coming to visit family for the holidays, but their parents' houses are too small and they don't want to stay in a hotel, so they're staying here. That's not our *target* demographic for these, but the income will be nice and Braden's hoping to generate some early online reviews for the townhomes to help promote the barn venue, once that's done."

"Sounds like Braden's been an excellent addition to the team," Uncle Jim said with a smile.

"He's been a big help," I said. "It's nice to have someone handle the books and all the other business things so I can focus on keeping the orchard healthy."

"Don't stray too far from the finances," Uncle Stan warned.

I nodded. "I know. I'm very protective of the finances and have frequent meetings with Braden about everything. We're partners and there's nothing he does without consulting me first."

"Good," Uncle Stan said.

Uncle Jim, meanwhile, was beaming. "You know, we're very proud of you. Your *parents* would be proud of you, too. As would your grandfather and great-grandfather."

Uncle Stan nodded in agreement. "You've really turned this place around."

"Thank you." I looked down at the ground, trying to hide how red my face was at the attention. "There's still work to be done. Chapman Farms isn't at the same level it used to be at. Not yet, at least."

"You'll get there," Uncle Jim assured me.

"I'm trying. I think with a lot of these changes that Braden's putting into place, and with my focus on maintaining the quality of our farm and our products, that we'll be able to buy back those parts of the business that we had to sell off…someday. Or maybe recreate them."

Uncle Stan raised his eyebrows. "That's a lofty goal."

"She'll do it," Uncle Jim said with confidence.

Again, I smiled at my uncles and turned to look back at the people lining up to enter the festival. This farm belonged to my family and, if I had anything to do with it, it would continue to be in our family for a long time. *That* would be my legacy.

# Behind the Book:
## *At the*
# CORE

The inspiration for this book came, unfortunately, from a true story. There is a local family-owned apple farm near Medina that needed to significantly reduce its operations because of changes in the economy, changes in their family, and changes in the apple market. That business was a staple for me and my family every time we went to Medina. Frustrated that yet another local business was impacted so negatively by things beyond their control, I wanted to write a happy ending to a fictionalized version of their story.

Except, when I started writing *At the Core*, Chapman Farms and the story of Autumn and Braden took on a life of its own, like it usually does once I get writing. While

there are still similarities that people local to Western New York may pick up on, I also took complete creative control whenever necessary,

Since the release of *Thanksgiving Day Parade*, I've been making a concerted effort to try to write a different kind of romance than what I had been writing with the Small Town Christmas series. Sure, it's all sweet romance and it all fits well under the D. Allen pen name, but I want to branch out and try to do more things with the pen name. Tell different types of stories. Lean more into the rom-com genre and try to recreate a bit of that juggernaut that was the late 90s/early 2000s romance movie genre. Except, obviously, with books.

In order to do that, I needed to do a little more research into how exactly to write that kind of romance. Just like with *Thanksgiving Day Parade*, I had a clear vision for this book. I knew I wanted to include tropes, I knew I wanted to have an illustrated cover, and I knew that I wanted a local setting. So I leaned on help from other successful romance authors, including looking at books that were popular at the time I was outlining this book in late 2024. (Social media posts about different romance books were a big draw for me while I was working on this book.)

And then, I shut out everything else I had been

looking at while I was writing and focused on the outline that I was drafting. And that's how *At the Core* began to take on a life of its own.

What I didn't expect was that this would become my longest D. Allen book to date. And I'm very proud of that. I originally set a modest goal, in terms of word count, but the story came to me so easily that before I knew it, I had blown through my original word count goal and nearly doubled it. I knew these characters very well and the writing just flowed. I hope that reading the book, you have a similar experience.

Thank you for supporting this book! Each time one of my books is read by a reader, it keeps me motivated to write another. Please consider leaving a review online once you're done, and consider even posting a picture of the book on social media.

If you liked this book, pick up
**Thanksgiving Day Parade**, another
sweet romance book!

DavidNethBooks.com/d-allen-
standalones

Julie Griffiths has had a crush on one of her friends at her hometown bar forever, but he's oblivious to her feelings. So when he and the rest of Julie's friends dare her to sneak into the Thanksgiving Day Parade in New York City, she accepts in order to impress her crush. Hours later, she finds herself on a crowded bus, equipped with nothing more than determination.

Brian Moore was already planning on going home to New York City for Thanksgiving, but a sudden breakup with his girlfriend gives him another reason. Heartbroken and lost, Brian isn't too happy when a woman sits beside him on the bus ride back to the city. Especially when she starts talking about her crazy idea to get into the Thanksgiving Day Parade.

Wanting to avoid an awkward encounter with his family, Brian agrees to help Julie accomplish her goal after it becomes painfully obvious that she has no plan for achieving it. But as the two begin to spend more time together, Julie starts to question her feelings for her friends back home while Brian realizes that maybe Julie is who he has been waiting for all along.

# Thanksgiving Day PARADE

## D. Allen

# Chapter One
## Thanksgiving Eve
### Julie

Some people spend the night before Thanksgiving putting together everything they'd need to prepare the big feast the following day. Others sit back and enjoy a night off. Perhaps some frantically clean their houses for the arrival of extended family, or maybe run to the grocery store to see if they can find any more canned cranberry sauce.

Me? I avoided all of that. As much as I could.

"I'll take my usual," I told the bartender at my favorite local hangout on South Pearl Street.

Jim popped the top off a bottle of beer and set it on the bar. "Want me to start a tab, Jules?"

I passed him my debit card and nodded. "Of course!"

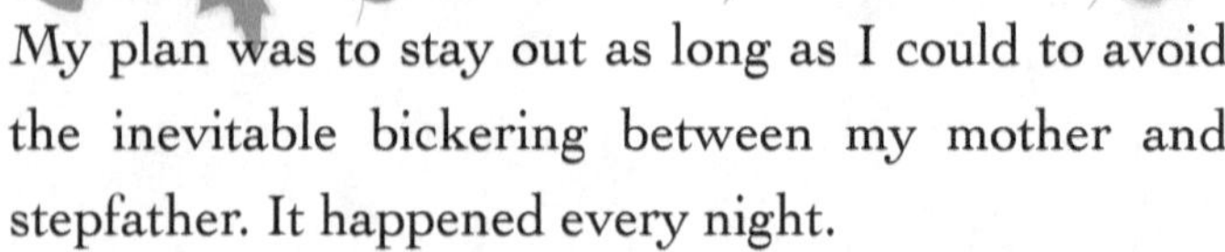

My plan was to stay out as long as I could to avoid the inevitable bickering between my mother and stepfather. It happened every night.

If it wasn't for the fact that she needed his salary to pay the mortgage and he needed her health insurance, I could pretty much guarantee the marriage would've crumbled a long time ago. Instead, they were trapped in this prison sentence, brought on by bureaucracy.

I've never been one for family time. We've never really been *tradition* people. Turkey and stuffing and going around the table to say how much we're thankful for wasn't really our thing.

The traditions I *did* enjoy, though? Spending time with people who are happy to see me. And after I snapped a quick picture of my beer bottle with the bar lights in the background, I grabbed it and stepped around the corner into the bowling alley, where three of my friends were just starting a game.

"Hey, cut me in!" I waved to my friends as I kicked off my shoes behind the bench and came around to greet them.

Brittany and Chloe both gave me hugs when they saw me. Eric was lined up like Fred Flintstone, all twinkle-toed and ready to hurl the ball down the lane. He did, and with a crash of pins, he tossed his hands up and roared, drawing all attention to him.

The lift of his shirt was hard to miss. He wasn't some muscle-chiseled model. His gut certainly showed that he liked beer. But his rugged handsomeness and overall charm made up for not having the perfect body. And that made my mind wonder about what the rest of his body looked like even more.

When he saw me, he cried out, "Julie!" and then wrapped his arm around me.

I put my arm around his bulk and leaned into him. His red beard tickled my face and some of my long blonde hair got tangled in it. I absently stroked my hair back into place when we parted, much sooner than I would've liked.

"You're late!" he said. "I've already got a strike on you!"

"We can add her in," Chloe said. "Each of us has only bowled once. Julie, if you want to play, it's your turn."

I nodded, then grabbed one of the balls in the return corral and stepped up to take my turn.

The marbled blue ball sailed down the lane and knocked out six pins. Not my best, but not my worst. I certainly needed warming up. My friends and I had tossed around the idea of joining a bowling league, but with me and Chloe being off to college and Brittany picking up as much overtime as she could manage, that really only left Eric and a few of our other drinking buddies, Tony and Otto. So, in a sense, the bowling league would have been a drinking league, making Eric and the other guys even more regulars of the bar than they already were.

"You're supposed to knock the pins down, Jules!" Eric cupped his hands around his mouth and shouted, as if he wasn't standing less than ten feet away from me. The hoarseness in his voice told me that he'd been shouting for a while. Clearly, he was already teetering on drunk. Factoring in his size and how often he drank, he must've started drinking at noon.

I tossed the ball down the lane a second time and knocked down two more pins. A total of eight. That was going to leave a mark on my score, compared to Eric's first-frame strike.

Chloe clapped her hands. "Good try, Jules!"

I retrieved my beer from the table, then found the picture I had taken of it on the bar and posted it to my Story. Then I snapped a picture of Brittany, who had stepped up to take her turn to bowl and posted that as well. Then, I leaned into Chloe and we both made kissing faces at the screen.

"Cute!" Chloe declared.

Another few presses on my screen, and that

picture was posted as well.

"Enough with the pictures, girls!" Eric said, with a fresh bottle of beer in his hand. "Jesus, this isn't a photoshoot."

I held up my phone and snapped one of him. He swiped at my phone and missed, resulting in a blurry picture of him. It looked artsy. I liked it.

"Sure, it is," I said. "Every day is a photo shoot!"

He tried again to take the phone from me, but I pulled it away in time, so he grabbed my wrist and spun me around so my back was pressed up against him. I giggled as we struggled, eventually sinking to the floor.

My heart fluttered with how close we were. There had been a lot more physical touches from Eric over the last couple months. I couldn't figure out whether he was flirting or not. Of course I wanted to *believe* that he was flirting, but my brain was telling me to put that wall up and not expect too much for fear of getting hurt.

"Looks like you're getting empty," Eric said.

My bottle was only halfway gone, but I recognized that it was an excuse to extract himself from the situation and avoid any further awkwardness.

Eric didn't do awkward.

In his absence, the game settled a bit. I took a seat next to Brittany while Chloe bowled.

"Are you dreading tomorrow as much as I am?" Brittany asked.

She had a perfectly normal family. A mom and a dad, two brothers, and even a family dog. But Brittany hated tradition and anything that made her feel normal. She felt trapped when she felt normal. Besides that, it was a forced day off from work for her, and when she was paid hourly, it mattered. She had wanted to go into work and get the holiday pay, but her mother had thrown a fit, so Brittany had no choice but to attend her traditional family Thanksgiving dinner, now laced with resentment between mother and daughter.

It wasn't quite the same situation as me, but it was still nice to commiserate with someone.

"Mm-hmm," I murmured. "Between my stepdad shouting at the stupid football game, my mother swearing and banging things around in the kitchen, and my brother being completely complacent to our messed up family, I would much rather skip the holiday."

"Right?" Brittany responded. "At least with Christmas we get gifts."

"*Then* there's a distraction," I said in agreement.

Chloe came back from the lane. "Where's Eric? He's up."

I nodded toward the bar. "Getting some refills. He'll be back."

"Again?" Chloe asked. "He just got another drink!"

Brittany nodded. "Just be glad Tony and Otto aren't here."

"Where are they again?" Chloe asked as she took a seat on the bench across from us.

"They're both traveling for Thanksgiving," Brittany said. "Tony's parents moved out to Tennessee—couldn't stand the New York taxes, I guess. Or maybe it was the weather. I don't know."

"And where's Otto?" I asked.

"They go up to his uncle's cabin in the Adirondacks every year for Thanksgiving to go hunting," she said. "The hunting season is a little different up there."

I nodded, then turned to my phone. "Well, it looks like Tony found a bar anyway." I leaned over and showed the girls a picture of Tony chugging from a beer can in some dark bar.

Chloe scoffed. "Typical." She was still nursing her first drink.

Brittany shrugged. "I mean, it *is* the night before Thanksgiving. That's, like, a drinking holiday. So I guess I get it today."

Chloe and I exchanged looks. We both disagreed

with Brittany about the drinking "holiday," but kept it to ourselves.

On one of the TVs hanging over the bowling lanes they were playing the nightly news. Was it the eleven o'clock? I had lost track of time. The footage showed a local marching band, while the words: LOCAL BAND TO MARCH IN THE THANKSGIVING DAY PARADE IN NYC scrolled across the bottom.

"Oh cool! One of the high school bands is going to be in the parade tomorrow." Chloe pointed to the screen. "Ugh, I can't wait to pour myself a cup of coffee and sit on the couch in my bathrobe and watch the parade with my sisters while the food cooks."

I nodded. "I do like the parade."

"I'm usually still passed out then," Brittany muttered. "If I'm going to have to take a day off, I better do it in a haze."

"I've always wanted to see it in person," I said, ignoring Brittany's comments.

"See what in person?" Eric asked as he came back with a pitcher of beer and plastic cups.

"The Thanksgiving Day Parade," I told him. "It would make the *perfect* Thanksgiving. Especially considering my Thanksgivings usually suck."

Brittany nodded. "That would be cool. I'd love to pass out the candy to the kids."

"I'd want to be on a float and wave to the kids," Chloe said.

Eric laughed. "Yeah, and I'd like to cut the ties to the balloons and let them all go."

The girls laughed, but I interjected a fun fact I had just learned about from a video I saw in my feed. "Actually, back in the day before they cared about pollution, that's exactly what they used to do with the big balloons."

"Now *that* would be something to see." Brittany pulled a plastic cup and filled it from the pitcher.

"Those streets are probably *mobbed*," Chloe said. "Could you imagine how long people are waiting just to get a glimpse of the parade?"

"Especially when you can just watch it at home in your underwear." Eric sloppily poured himself another drink.

"I don't know," I said, trying to get the image of Eric in his underwear out of my head. "The parade route is a couple miles long. I think the crowd might not be that bad. It's not like it's New Year's Eve or anything."

"Still, those floats probably have to be registered *way* in advance," Chloe said. "I wonder if there's a waiting list to get in the parade. Or a fee—I'm sure there's a fee. There's always a fee with everything nowadays."

"Free marketing," I added. "But I'm not sure it'd be terribly hard to get on one. I see random people on those floats next to celebrities and characters all the time."

Chloe shook her head. "They're not random, Jules. They're probably a part of the team for that float—someone who works for the company but doesn't have camera time. Someone who isn't a household name. I think half the time the celebrities are the ones who are random just so they can help advertise the parade."

"Which then advertises the company." Brittany rolled her eyes. "It's all a big marketing scam, and we're falling into it."

I turned back to the TV, which had moved on to a statement about new street parking rules for the upcoming winter season.

I didn't want to believe that the parade was just a marketing gimmick. I mean, yes, of course, that was the main purpose when the parade had first started, but since then it had evolved into so much more than that. A sense of community for the whole country, which spawned millions of tiny moments of families creating traditions and memories around it over the last several decades.

"Either way," Chloe said, breaking into my thoughts. "Those people on the floats aren't just nobodies. They're real people, working hard for their companies, who deserve to be in the limelight, even if for only a few seconds a year."

"They might as well be nobodies," Eric said. "I don't know them and I don't give a shit about any of them. I don't even watch the parade. No point."

"Would you watch it if you knew someone in the parade?" I asked him.

He scoffed. "Yeah, like *that's* ever going to happen!"

The idea of Eric watching the parade at home in his underwear, as he so eloquently stated, was still stuck in my head.

"I'm just saying, I don't think it'd be that hard to get on a float," I said. "I could do it."

Brittany narrowed her eyes. She was growing skeptical of my bravado. "Okay, well, if it's not that hard then why haven't you done it?"

I averted my eyes. Where was I going with that statement anyway? It wasn't like I was ever going to get to be in the parade. Especially not when there was less than twelve hours before it started.

"Oh, I bet you could do it." Eric wrapped his arm around me and tugged me closer.

The physical touch made my heart race, but also left disappointment seeping through my veins. He gave me the awkward side-hug that he gave to everyone whenever he had had several drinks in him.

Chloe rolled her eyes. "None of you are listening to me. All of this is decided on *well* in advance! They're not just seat-fillers walking down the street in one of the biggest parades in the country!"

"In fact," Eric went on, clearly ignoring Chloe. "I *dare* you to get on a float."

Brittany broke out into a wide grin and *oohed*. "Oh man! Now you *have* to do it!" It was possible that Brittany had had too much to drink as well. "Wait, wait, wait!" She pulled out her phone and began recording me. "Julie Griffiths, do you accept the dare to get on a float in the Thanksgiving Day Parade by the end of the parade tomorrow morning?"

I froze. I couldn't turn the dare down. Not with their scrutinizing eyes on me. Not with it being recorded—which I knew would be posted immediately with my handle being tagged. Everyone online would see it as well.

"Jules, you don't have to," Chloe said from beside Brittany.

"Of course she does!" Eric blurted. "She's been *dared*."

Another moment passed, then I recovered and put on some confidence—even though it was fake. "What's my reward if I do it?"

There were several more *oohs* from around. The group of guys bowling next to us had taken interest in our conversation. Not sure how, being that Brittany and Eric were making me a spectacle and all.

Eric considered my question, then said, "I'll pay for your drinks for the rest of your life—*if* you can pull it off."

Another round of *oohs* erupted from the peanut gallery.

If Eric was my drink bitch for the rest of my life, then I would have a reason to call him up out of the blue to come and buy me a drink. I would have a reason to text him, to tease him, to spend more time with him. But I needed to make it more personal. "I need at least one meal a week in there, too."

"Greedy, huh?" Eric asked with a smirk.

I smiled back, playful. Pushing the limits of our game of cat and mouse. "Hey, a girl's gotta eat."

"Fine." Eric stuck out his hand. "*If* you can do it, you'll have one meal a week on me and drinks for life."

I smiled and shook his hand. "Then you have a deal."

# Chapter Two
## Thanksgiving Eve
### Brian

"Babe, stop!" Kendra sobbed as she tugged on Brian's arm.

He ignored her and continued to shove as many of his clothes into a single duffel bag as he could fit. There were so many other things that were his throughout the apartment, but those would have to wait. Right now he just needed to get out.

"Won't you please *talk* to me?" she pleaded.

With effort, he zipped up his bag. It was nearly bursting at the seams. When he finally got it zipped closed, he slung it over his shoulder and brushed past her through the bedroom door.

"I'm sorry!" she wailed. "Brian, I'm sorry! I'm sorry I

messed everything up. If I could go back and change it all, I would!"

He stopped in the bathroom and grabbed his toothbrush and retainers—nothing about this was the clean getaway that he had been hoping for. But then, reality was usually different than TV. The truth of the matter was, without the retainers he had gotten at sixteen, the gap between his two front teeth would rear its ugly head within two days.

Salt in the wound.

His computer lay on the table beside the couch. He scooped it up and tried to find a place in his bag to shove it in. Everything was jam packed. And then there was his charger. He unplugged it from the wall, but felt resistance on the other end.

Kendra.

She looked at him with red, puffy, wet eyes, and held onto the other end of his charger. "I won't let you go until you talk to me."

He pulled on the cord, but she refused to let it go.

"Please, Brian," she said. "Stay here so we can talk this out."

Another shot against her. She had clearly forgotten that he had planned to go back home for Thanksgiving anyway. The bus ticket had been booked weeks ago. The implosion of their relationship had only removed the necessity of missing each other.

Her dark hair hung limply around her face, which was swollen and wet with tears. She really was an ugly crier. "I love you. I never wanted to hurt you."

The rage he had been shoving down erupted inside him, spilling out of his mouth.

"That's a lie!" He pointed right at her face. "You knew exactly what you were doing. So don't sit there and pretend like you didn't expect all of this to happen."

"I know! You're right! It was a mistake! I know that. But that doesn't mean we need to give up on this. On us."

"What part of my reaction came as a surprise, Kendra? Huh?" He raised his eyebrows, waiting for an answer, but none came.

"I'm sorry," she said.

"You're sorry you got caught. You *might* even be sorry that you hurt me. But you're not sorry for what you did, because you knew what you were doing all along. You made the choice, Kendra. Now you have to live with it. So all of this guilt and shame you feel, you deserve it." With another tug on the cord, it slipped from her hands.

"Okay—okay! I'm a terrible person! I did this to myself. You're right. You're right about all of it. But can't you give me a second chance? Can't we make this work?"

He wasn't sure there was any recovering from this scar in their relationship. Nor did he care to find out. He could hardly stand to look Kendra in the face for another second without seeing what she had done.

"Goodbye, Kendra," he said simply.

Without another word, he gathered his overstuffed bag, laptop, and cord, and stepped out of the apartment into the hallway, slamming the door behind him.

It wasn't until he made it down to the lobby that he found a bench nearby and opened his bag to move things around. He shoved his laptop and charging cord inside, then put his weight on it while he forced the zipper to close. It pulled at the seams, but held.

There was a train stop not far from their apartment — Kendra's apartment now. He didn't live there anymore.

He got on the train, rode it downtown to Union Station, then got in line to board a bus to New York City. A nine hour ride. One that would travel overnight, thankfully.

Toronto was the start of the bus line, so when he and the other passengers got on, they all had plenty of room in their seats. That would change with each city they stopped in along the way to the Big Apple.

Brian set his bag on the empty seat next to him,

then put up his hood and leaned against the window as it pulled away from the station.

The intent was to sleep, but his mind was spinning with having his whole world turned upside down that he knew sleep would be impossible.

He would have to move back home. Back in with his mother until he could find a place on his own. And, depending on how long it took him to extract his life from Kendra's, his mother would be his roommate for a while until he saved enough to rent his own apartment. And it wasn't like real estate in New York was cooling down anytime soon.

He would have to notify work, tell them he was coming back into the office after spending the last year working remotely. He would have to arrange another trip back to Toronto to get the rest of his stuff from the apartment. Clothes, books, several dishes, food he had helped pay for.

On second thought, he realized it was all replaceable. Anything of sentimental or significant monetary value was stuffed into the duffel bag beside him. His whole world crammed into one small little bag.

The bus slowed as the lanes in the road narrowed for the checkpoint to cross the border. Yet another step forward toward home. Toward his new life. Toward his family.

How was he going to break the news to his family? His mother adored Kendra. His brothers got along nicely with her. They had all talked about vacationing together, seeing each other for the holidays, and even doing other things together.

Thanksgiving dinner was going to be awkward.

Brian shifted in his seat as the bus lurched forward, then braked again, then lurched forward yet again. Inching forward little-by-little until the driver was finally given the approval to enter the country.

That was another thing on his to-do list: talk to immigration about ending his Canadian visa early. Brian shook his head in disappointment—embarrassment. He would have to be reminded of the things he had done to make things work with Kendra. The lengths he had gone to for that woman. All in the name of love. What a crock that turned out to be.

Not only had he moved away from his family, but he had moved to a whole different *country*—they had even discussed him applying for dual citizenship when the two of them got married.

Yeah. That definitely wouldn't be happening.

In another thirty minutes, the bus pulled up to the first stop in the United States: Buffalo.

Brian sat back and pretended he was asleep,

hoping that nobody would be willing to wake him to claim the seat beside him. Besides, it was the first stop so there were still plenty of other seats that people could take. The tactic had worked on previous trips home.

The noise level on the bus increased as people found their seats, but fifteen minutes later everyone settled. And Brian still had an empty seat beside him. At least he'd be able to get *some* sleep until the next stop in Rochester.

It was late. The overnight trips were usually not as popular as the daytime ones. Most people were more willing to sacrifice a perfectly good day in order to travel than they were to sacrifice a good night's sleep.

Brian cracked his eyes open, chancing a glance at the front. The driver was back in his seat and pulling on his seatbelt.

Home free.

Brian closed his eyes and settled back into his seat. He tried to get comfortable again, but then he heard someone talking at the front. Probably passengers trying to get comfortable and discuss seating arrangements with the strangers they needed to sit by. Brian didn't focus on what they were saying.

The bus began to pull away.

Someone nudged his shoulder. "Excuse me. Can

you please move your bag? There aren't any other seats."

His eyes flicked open and he saw a girl standing there. Probably only a few years younger than him. She had a large purse on her shoulder and she stood holding the back of the seat to steady her.

She was beautiful. Blonde hair that hung around her face, and clear blue eyes that seemed to shine, even in the nighttime dark.

But the last thing he needed at the moment was to be admiring another woman. He just wanted to be alone—to disappear from the world for a couple hours. But so far, being alone had only left him trapped by his thoughts. Maybe a passenger would help him focus on other things than letting his mind run rampant on the journey home.

"Lady, let's go! Take a seat!" the driver called from the front.

The girl turned to him with those perfect blue eyes, pleading.

Brian grumbled and sat up, pulling his heavy bag onto his lap. As the girl settled in beside him, Brian felt even more cramped in the window seat.

Between the tight confines and his running thoughts, there was certainly going to be no sleeping tonight.

# Chapter Three
## Thanksgiving Eve
### Julie

The seats were so uncomfortable. I tried several times to readjust, finding minimal comfort on my side. The problem was, when I lay like that, I was too close to the guy sitting next to me, who was *clearly* not happy about having to share his seat.

As if it was my fault.

Finally, I got too tired of trying to get comfortable and resigned myself to the idea that I wouldn't be sleeping, like I'd hoped. Whatever alcohol I'd had at the bar had worn off. Eric, Brittany, and—begrudgingly—Chloe all chipped in for my Uber to the airport, where the Buffalo bus stop was. I had just managed to arrive by midnight, when the bus was about to pull away. Luckily,

I had the ticket information on my phone and the driver let me on.

Throughout the bus, everyone was quiet, even though it seemed that nobody could properly get to sleep. Sure, most people had their eyes closed and were *trying*, but the way each of them moved every few seconds said that their efforts were futile.

Even the guy sitting next to me was tossing and turning, trying to find a way to get comfortable sitting upright in his seat with his bag sitting in his lap.

I felt guilty for taking the empty seat next to him but it was the last one.

Well, actually, no. It wasn't the last one. There were two up near the front. One next to a guy who looked a little *too* excited at the prospect of a young college girl sitting next to him, and one next to a woman who had enough B.O. to fill the front of the bus.

That left the semi-attractive guy in the back. The one who very much did not want to share his seat. Too bad.

My phone rang, and several people turned and gave me dirty looks. I silenced it, then looked around. There were no signs that said that talking *wasn't* allowed. And it wasn't like I was going to talk as loud as I could.

So I answered.

"Hey," Chloe said on the other end. "I wanted to talk to you about that dare. I know we chipped in to Uber you to the airport, and I know you bought a ticket, but…" She took a deep breath. "Don't do it, Jules. It was just a stupid joke that Eric made. One he's probably not even going to remember in the morning. Currently, he's passed out in a booth in the bar."

It was quiet on the other end, so I assumed that Chloe stepped outside to make the call. It was kind of strange to think that they were still at the bar and I was on my way to the biggest city in the country in the middle of the night.

"Well, even if I *did* want to turn around, Chloe, your timing is terrible," I said. "I'm already on the bus. We already left."

Chloe was quiet for minute, followed only by a single, "Oh."

"Yeah," I murmured. The lady across the aisle from me continued to glare at me. As if my phone call was bothering her ability to listen to her earbuds. I was talking quietly, and the roar of the bus motor was loud enough as it was.

"Look, I'll split the bus fare with you if you want to get on a bus right away to come back," Chloe offered. "Or if you get off at the next city, I can drive out and pick you up. I've only had one, so I'd be okay to drive."

"No, Chloe, I don't want you to risk it. Besides, this is something I want to do. I bet you the first thing Eric asks when he wakes up is where the remote is so he can watch it on TV." There was more silence on the other end, so I added, "Come on, Chloe! You and I both know I dread any holiday with my family. It's not like I'm missing anything with this one. Let me make this Thanksgiving a memorable one."

Chloe sighed again. "I can't talk you out of this?"

"I don't think so."

"And you're going to be safe?"

"I promise."

"And you'll call me if you get into trouble?"

"Anytime."

"And you'll have fun?"

I cracked a smile. "That's the plan."

"Then I guess I can't stop you. Be careful, Jules."

"I will. Thanks, Chloe."

I tucked my phone back in my bag and then tried to relax. Chloe had given me an out and I stuck firm with my decision.

But was it the right one? I had never even been to New York City. Maybe Chloe was right. Maybe I should just get off in Rochester and call for a ride home.

Of course, if I called my mother, I would have to be subjected to the wrath of her and my stepdad, making Thanksgiving dinner even more unbearable than I had already expected it to be. Not to mention the endless scrutiny from my brother. And I would never be able to show my face in the bar again. Any chance at anything more with Eric would certainly be out the window. I should've suggested that he and I both come to get on the float instead of jetting off by myself and leaving him alone with Brittany.

How stupid was I?

Nope. I wasn't going to go there. I needed to change my thoughts. I *would* be successful at this. And if I wasn't? I'd have one hell of a story to tell.

The guy beside me shifted in his seat again. He clearly was not catching any Zs. When he turned and saw me looking at him, he scrunched his eyebrows together as if to say, "What are you looking at?"

Instead, I smiled and offered my hand. "Hi, I'm Julie."

He glared at me, but sat up straighter, adjusting the bag in his lap, then pulled his hood off and shook my hand. "I'm Brian." He turned back to the window, not engaging in anymore conversation.

"Where are you headed to?" I asked.

"New York," he murmured, eyes still trained out the window. We couldn't see much in the darkness.

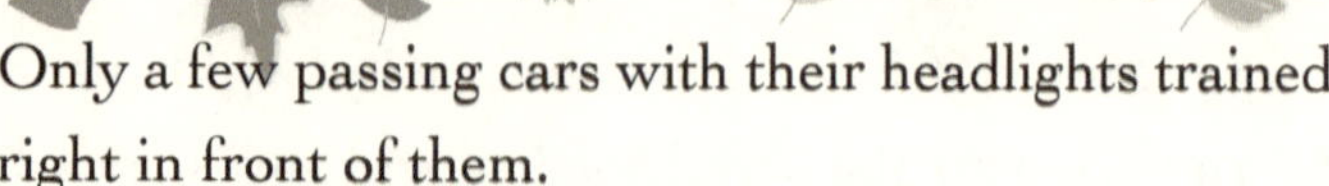

Only a few passing cars with their headlights trained right in front of them.

"Oh wow! That's where I'm going too! Are you going for the parade?"

Another glare in my direction, then, "No, I'm going home for Thanksgiving."

My eyes widened. "You *live* in New York City?" My voice was louder than I expected and several people around us cleared their throats, which had nothing to do with the chillier temperatures springing up illnesses.

Of course I knew that New York City had a population of over eight million people, but I hadn't really met anyone my own age from there. Sure, I had met people from *down state* in college, but they seemed to be from the outskirts of "the city."

Or maybe it was that they told me the names of places within the city and I just didn't know where those places were. Until Eric had challenged me, I had had no real interest in going to New York City. So much had changed in such little time.

"Uh…yeah, I guess that's where I live now." He seemed to sober as he considered my question. With his hood off, I could see that he was more than just *semi*-attractive. Still, his attitude was off-putting.

"You guess?" I asked. "Are you, like, moving or something?"

Another pause as he considered. "Yeah, I guess I am." He turned his body back toward the window, quietly telling me that he didn't want to talk.

That never bothered me. I laughed a little to myself. "You guess a lot."

He shrugged.

I fiddled with the strap on my bag. "Well, I'm going to New York City on a dare to see if I can get on a float in the parade."

Brian looked over at me. "You mean the big televised one?"

"Mm-hmm," I said with a nod.

"You're crazy."

Now it was my turn to shrug. As he continued to look at me with wild eyes, I laughed again. "I know I'm crazy. And that this idea is a little wild—"

"A *little* wild?"

"What's the worst that can happen?"

"The worst that can happen is that you get arrested."

My lips formed into a giant *O* as the realization hit me. *Of course* there would security and police patrolling throughout the parade. Any violators, no matter how innocent, would have to face legal repercussions. Was I making a mistake? I supposed it was too late to back down now.

Brian sighed and sat up. "Here's what you need to do: find a float that has costumed characters—but only the ones who stand and wave. You don't want the ones who have to dance or anything. Then, if you can convince one of them to let you wear their costume instead of them, you can sneak on the float undetected."

"You think it's that easy?"

"I wouldn't say it's *easy*, but I think that's your best bet. Those people in the costumes probably go to the parade every year. All they want is the paycheck. As long as you're not taking that from them, then sure, I think you could swing it."

I smirked, glad that I hooked him into a conversation so I didn't have to sit alone. "The trouble is, in order for me to win the dare, my friends need to be able to see me on camera. If I put on a character costume, they won't be able to see me unless I take the costume off—and scar millions of children watching in the process."

Brian laughed at that. "Who even proposed this dare?"

Now it was my turn to look away. "Just a friend of mine."

"Well, it sounds like they were setting you up to fail by creating all of these rules."

"He didn't set *rules*," I blurted. "But it makes

sense that he needs to be able to see me in order to know I was there."

"He can't just take your word for it?"

My shoulders began to raise up. "Well...I don't know..."

"Sounds to me like you could've snapped a few pictures and sent them as proof enough. Your friend doesn't trust that you won't cheat?"

"Okay, *stranger*, you don't need to be critiquing my life—and my *friends*, who you don't even know!"

"Fine, I won't critique your friends, but I'll critique their stupid idea. It's stupid."

I raised my eyebrows. "Wow. What a great comeback."

"I'm not really sure how to dumb it down anymore."

I rolled my eyes. Now I was regretting striking up a conversation with this arrogant jerk. "Never mind." I turned away from him and focused on the man who was sleeping three rows up. It looked like he was about to fall out of his seat and into the aisle. I wondered how many bumps in the road or sudden turns it would take to get him to topple over.

"Look," Brian said from beside me. "I'm sorry for saying this idea is stupid—don't get me wrong, I still think that. I'm just sorry for saying it out loud."

"Is this supposed to be an apology?"

"Of sorts. If you're really dead-set on doing this, I guess I can help you figure out how."

"Really?" I was suddenly more excited than I expected. The burden of having to figure it all out on my own had been weighing on me and I didn't even realize it until someone offered relief. I didn't know the city. I didn't know how the parade was planned. I didn't know how I was going to pull this off. I didn't really know anything.

He nodded. "Yep. You need a new plan."

"That's it? That's your big advice?"

"Can you blame me? I've never even thought of doing something so stupid before. And you've given me—what?—five minutes to figure this out for you?"

I rolled my eyes again and turned back to the man about to topple over. His neck was jarred in such an uncomfortable position that I wondered briefly if he might be dead. But then he snorted and shifted a little, proving that life was still present. A Thanksgiving miracle.

"Let me think about this," Brian muttered from beside me. "Maybe you can hang around the parade starting point to look for an opening."

I looked over at him. "The parade starting point?"

"Well, yeah. It has to start somewhere, right?"

"I guess I never really thought about it. But sure,

that sounds about right."

He narrowed his eyes. "You haven't put any thought into this at all, have you?"

"I've known about this for—" I checked the time on my phone. "—only about three hours!"

"You were only dared three hours ago and now you're on a bus across the state? That's a little…impulsive."

I shrugged. "Sometimes you have to be impulsive. That's where the best stories come from, right?"

He didn't say anything, but the expression on his face said enough. He was judging me. Hardcore.

Then again, even I could agree that this plan, in hindsight, *was* kind of stupid. But my pride wouldn't let me admit that out loud.

"Yes, there's a parade starting point," Brian went on. "If you head up there, they're probably using some of the park to—"

"Central Park," I cut in, boasting my little knowledge of New York City.

"Yes…" he said slowly, then added, "Do you have any idea where the parade route starts?"

"Central Park," I said with a proud smile.

"You do realize that Central Park stretches, like, fifty blocks, right? It's huge."

"And?"

"And you can't just say it starts at the park, you

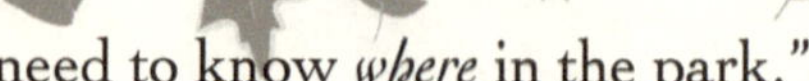

need to know *where* in the park."

"Do *you* know where?" I pressed. Mr. Smarty-Pants was flaunting his knowledge now. I wasn't a dumb girl. Okay, sure, maybe this trip wasn't my most shining example of a *good* idea, but I was certainly smarter than it seemed.

"Central Park West and 78th Street," he said. "Near the museum."

"And you just *happened* to know that?"

He looked a little defensive. "I was reading an article about it the other day and I thought it was interesting."

A man who read. Who had ever heard of that?

"Do you have any idea where that is?" he asked.

"The park!" I said with a laugh.

He closed his eyes, took a deep breath, and gently nodded. "Yes. By the park. Have you even been to New York before?"

"I live in New York," I said.

"I meant New York *City*."

"Oh! No."

He shook his head. "You're going to need more help than just coming up with a plan."

I smiled. "You seem like you know your way around town, being that you're a New Yorker and all. Why don't you help me?" As I said the words, I wondered if I would regret them. Then again, it wasn't as if I hadn't been around arrogance before. My defense mechanism to that was to deflect to humor.

"I don't…" he started, but then stopped when my face began to droop with disappointment. It hadn't been my intent to guilt him into it, but I couldn't help the look on my face as all my wildest dreams came crashing down with his denial.

We were quiet as the proposal, and the beginning of a rejection, hung in the air between us.

Finally, he said, "Okay. I'll help you. But you need to trust my advice."

"Done."

"And you need to listen."

"We'll see."

"And if the police start poking around, I'm out."

"Understandable." I smiled again and offered my hand for the second time. "So…do we have a deal?"

He let out a heavy breath of air, then took my hand. "Fine. Deal."

It was the second deal I made that night. But I felt good about this one.

TO READ THE REST OF **THANKSGIVING DAY PARADE**,
ORDER YOUR COPY AT
DAVIDNETHBOOKS.COM/D-ALLEN-STANDALONES

# THANK YOU

Thank you to the DN Publishing VIP Club members over at Patreon! Become a member and enjoy weekly perks!

Tracy O'Neil

Marguerite Goosby


patreon.com/DNPublishing

# ACKNOWLEDGMENTS

This project would not have been possible without the support of my Kickstarter backers! Thank you all for your support!

John Idlor
Backer 2
Julie McAtee
Heiko Koenig
Ashley Webster
Marguerite G
Christy S
E. R. Paskey
Kanyon N.
Franchesca Caram
Kay Leyda
Brittni Chenelle
Backer 13
Marlene Renteria
Florentina
Giselle T.

Ellis St. Kaye of Ellis Kaye Creates
Stacey Andrews
Ashli Montgomery
A. Sturniolo
Kaitlyn Mehrtens
Mary Mensah
Natalie Munford
Christopher McGee
Christina Schlickenmeyer
Chantelle-Emma Hilton
Morgan G.
Laura L
Rachael Barcellano
Amanda Balter
Gary Phillips

Jessie moved back to picturesque Montana Beach after a heartbreaking split with her ex. She's since thrown herself into her grandparent's inn, which has been struggling financially thanks to the town having seen better days. With few options available, Jessie considers accepting a developer's offer to buy Montana Manor, seeing it as a way to save her family's legacy, until she learns that he wants to tear it down.

Meanwhile, Mason's tired of working at his father's advertising firm in New York City, although his father wants him to become his replacement. Unsure if that's the course he wants his life to take, Mason escapes to Montana Beach and the only inn in town to consider the proposal. But after he meets Jessie, he seems to gain only another reason not to take up his father's offer.

When Mason offers to help Jessie launch a campaign to save Montana Manor, the two quickly find themselves relying more and more on each other. But summer doesn't last forever, and Mason's stay is coming to an end.

*Summer Stay* is the first book in the Montana Beach series. Available in hardcover, paperback, ebook, and audiobook!

www.DavidNethBooks.com/MontanaBeach

A chance moment. A snow storm. And the gift of a new beginning.

Tristan is ready to party and ring in the New Year by kissing his soon-to-be girlfriend, Julie. The only bad note in his rocking night is the ongoing snow storm. Outside his apartment, he's almost hit by a swerving car! Behind the wheel is Grace, the most beautiful woman with haunting green eyes. She's on her own mission to get home to her grandfather.

In a selfless act reminiscent of the age of knights and chivalry, Tristan vows to get her home…never realizing they are both on a date with destiny and their lives will be forever changed by the SNOW AFTER CHRISTMAS…

www.DavidNethBooks.com/d-allen-standalones

# More by the author

To find more books by the author, visit
DavidNethBooks.com/Books

* * *

Subscribe to his newsletter to be the first to know of new
releases and special deals!
DavidNethBooks.com/Newsletter

* * *

If you enjoyed the book, please consider leaving a review
on Goodreads or the retailer you bought it from. Reviews
help potential readers determine whether they'll enjoy a
book, so any comments on what you thought of the story
would be very helpful!

# About the Author

D. Allen is the author of the sweet small town romance series, Montana Beach and Small Town Christmas.

Also writes fantasy and superhero fiction as David Neth.

www.DavidNethBooks.com
www.facebook.com/DavidNethBooks
www.instagram.com/dnpublishing
www.patreon.com/DNPublishing